Stacey and the Mystery at the Mall

Other Books by
Ann M. Martin

Rachel Parker, Kindergarten Show-off

Eleven Kids, One Summer

Ma and Pa Dracula

Yours Turly, Shirley

Ten Kids, No Pets

Slam Book

Just a Summer Romance

Missing Since Monday

With You and Without You

Me and Katie (the Pest)

Stage Fright

Inside Out

Bummer Summer

BABY-SITTERS LITTLE SISTER series
THE BABY-SITTERS CLUB mysteries
THE BABY-SITTERS CLUB series
(see back of book for a more complete listing)

Stacey and the Mystery at the Mall
Ann M. Martin

AN
APPLE
PAPERBACK

SCHOLASTIC INC.
New York Toronto London Auckland Sydney

The author gratefully acknowledges
Ellen Miles
for her help in
preparing this manuscript.

Cover art by Hodges Soileau

ISBN 0-590-47052-3

12 11 10 9 8 7 6 5 4 3 2 1   4 5 6 7 8 9/9

Printed in the U.S.A.   40

First Scholastic printing, April 1994

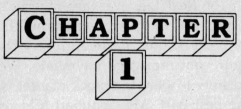

CHAPTER 1

"Terrific work, Stacey," said Mr. Schubert, handing back my final report. "According to your summaries, you've earned so much in the stock market that you could retire in — oh, about two years."

I giggled. "Right," I said. "I'll move to Miami at the ripe old age of fifteen." I looked at the front page of my report, which had a big, red A+ at the top of it. It wasn't my first A or anything (I'm a pretty decent student), but I felt especially proud of it. I've always been good at math, but this class was something new. Math for Real Life, it was called. It was part of a program at school called Short Takes, in which all the students in every grade take the same special class. This is how it works: you study a subject intensively for a short period of time, and you learn awesome stuff that isn't usually taught in school. For instance, one really cool Short Takes class was

Modern Living, in which pairs of students had to "adopt" an egg and pretend it was their baby. We've also had Career Class, and special health and civics classes.

Math for Real Life was my favorite Short Takes class yet. In it, we had learned how to balance a checkbook, make a grocery budget, and figure out mortgage payments. We also learned how to play the stock market, which was the best part. Mr. Schubert told us that we each had (an imaginary) five thousand dollars to invest, and then he showed us how to read the financial pages and pick out stocks to buy. The report I had just gotten back showed the results of my investing, which were pretty impressive, if I do say so myself.

I'm Stacey McGill, and the school I go to is Stoneybrook Middle School, which is in Stoneybrook, Connecticut. I'm thirteen and in the eighth grade, which is why I cracked up when Mr. Schubert said I could retire in two years. I'm nowhere *near* ready for retirement. I have a long, exciting life in front of me, and there are lots of things I want to do before I start spending my days in a rocking chair. I don't know what I want to be "when I grow up," as we used to say in first grade, but lately I've been thinking about going to business school and becoming a trader on the stock exchange!

Mr. Schubert makes that sound pretty exciting.

Another thing I think I'd be good at is running a small company — or even a big one. I'd love to own a chain of stores, for example. My math skills would come in handy, and so would my shopping skills. I'm an *excellent* shopper. This is partly because I grew up in New York City, which is like shopper's heaven. If you want or need anything, you can find it in New York, usually at half price. I know how to track down all the bargains, whether I'm in New York or Stoneybrook. I love fashion, for example; I really enjoy dressing in trendy, sophisticated outfits. But I don't just buy the first thing I see. I make a game of it: shopping around, checking prices, figuring out how to get the most for my money. Like, when I see a pair of jeans I want, I note the cost and move on. I have this little place in my brain where I remember the prices of the things I've seen, so it's easy for me to figure out where to get the best value.

On the other hand, money and math and clothes aren't the only things I care about. I love to go to museums, and dance performances and Broadway shows, and yes, even the opera. (Well, not *all* operas.) I guess I'm a "culture vulture" — another result of growing up in Manhattan. My parents were always dragging me to one event or another, and eventually I learned to appreciate and love the arts.

That may be part of the reason my best friend, Claudia Kishi, and I get along so well. I'm a patron of the arts (at least, that's what my dad calls it), and Claudia's an artist. She doesn't just draw or paint; she also sculpts, makes collages, and creates all kinds of "wearable art." Give her some raw materials — a few beads, some clay, a tube or two of paint — and she'll come up with a masterpiece.

Claudia also shares my love of fashion. She believes clothes should do more than cover our bodies and keep us warm. Instead, she sees dressing as one more creative outlet, and it shows. She always looks fabulous, and she *never* looks just like everyone else. She'll pair a long white shirt with a colorful vest, accessorize with handmade jewelry, pull her hair up into an outrageous ponytail, and look like a million dollars.

Claud's gorgeous to begin with, anyway. She's Japanese-American and very exotic-looking, with her long black hair and almond-shaped eyes. On the other hand, I'm your basic blue-eyed blonde. The other differences between me and Claud? For starters, she thinks being in math class is like being in a torture chamber. School is not Claudia's favorite thing, to say the least. (Her older sister Janine is a certified genius. Honest! Teachers are probably always wishing they had higher grades than A+ to give to Janine.)

For another thing, Claudia is the Junk Food Queen of Stoneybrook. Give her a Ring-Ding, and she's happy. Add a couple of Three Musketeers bars, and she's in heaven. Me? I don't eat the stuff. Not because I don't like it — I do. But I have diabetes, and I have to be very, very careful about every single thing I eat. Sweets are out. See, diabetes is this disease in which your body doesn't deal well with sugar. This has to do with an organ called the pancreas, but I don't really want to get into that right now. Basically, I'm all right as long as I follow my diet carefully and take shots of insulin every day. I give the shots to myself, which sounds much worse than it is. I'm used to it. I'd better be, since I'll probably have to do it for the rest of my life.

"People! People, please settle down." Mr. Schubert had finished passing out our papers, and he was standing in front of the room trying to get our attention. Everybody was comparing papers and talking excitedly about how much money they'd made — or lost — in the stock market. This boy, Pete Hayes, was joking about how there should be one last

5

topic in Math for Real Life, called "How to File for Bankruptcy."

Finally, we quieted down and looked at Mr. Schubert. "This has been a great class," he said. "I've enjoyed teaching you all, and I'll miss you when you go on to your next Short Takes class next week."

"What's it going to be?" somebody yelled out. "Zoo-keeping? How to Be a Clown?"

They never tell us about the next Short Takes course until the week before, which means it's always a surprise. Some other kids jumped in with funny ideas.

"Advanced Skateboard Riding?" Pete Hayes called out.

"How To Drive Your Little Sister Crazy?" asked somebody else.

Soon we were all cracking up. Even Mr. Schubert was laughing. Then he held up his hands for silence. "Give me a chance, and I'll tell you," he said. As soon as we all shut up, he announced, "The next Short Takes is called Project Work."

Everybody groaned.

"What, like doing chores around the house?" asked Erica Blumberg, who was sitting in front of me. "I don't need a class to teach me how to take out the garbage or rake the lawn."

I had to admit Project Work didn't sound

6

like a whole lot of fun. But I listened to Mr. Schubert anyway. "For Project Work," he went on, "every student at SMS will go out into the community after school three days a week and actually work in a business of his or her choice."

"Cool," said Erica. "So we can, like, make a bunch of money and get school credit at the same time?"

"Well, not exactly," said Mr. Schubert. "You won't be getting paid. The idea is for you to pick a place that interests or excites you, and find out what it's really like to work there. It's called hands-on experience. We have a wide variety of businesses for you to choose from, some in Stoneybrook, some in Stamford, and some at the Washington Mall."

I, for one, was getting interested. Project Work sounded as if it could be fun. As I said, I've often thought I'd like to run a store — maybe this was my chance to see what it was like.

"The good news," Mr. Schubert said next, "is that there won't be any homework assignments or tests." A cheer went up. "You'll have to keep a journal, and Mr. Withum, your next teacher, will tell you more about that."

I started to think about what kind of work I might be able to do. I knew my mom would have some good ideas. She's a buyer at Bellair's, a department store in downtown Stoneybrook. She took the job after my parents got divorced. That was a hard time for me, the divorce. Here's how it happened. I had grown up in New York, but then my dad was transferred to Stoneybrook, so we moved here. I made friends right away and joined this great club called the BSC — the Baby-sitters Club. But then my dad was transferred back to New York, and I had to say good-bye to all my new friends. Bummer. But an even bigger bummer was coming my way.

Soon after we moved back to the city, my parents started to fight a lot. Now, a lot of parents fight, and it doesn't necessarily mean they're going to get a divorce. But in my parents' case, it did. When they decided to split up, my mom told me she planned to move back to Stoneybrook. My dad was staying in New York. And guess what? I had to choose which one of them I wanted to live with. It was the hardest thing I've ever had to do. Obviously, I chose to come back to Stoneybrook with my mom, and I have never regretted the decision. I visit my dad as often as possible, and I still feel close to him. But Stoneybrook is my home now. It may not have Bloomingdale's or Carnegie Hall, but I love it anyway.

The bell rang, and Mr. Schubert smiled at

us. "Enjoy Project Work!" he said. "I know you'll have a great time."

Since Short Takes is my last class of the day, I headed for my locker as soon as we were dismissed. When I reached it, I found a note stuck into the vents. I could tell at a glance that it was from Claudia. She always decorates her notes with swirls and moons and stars. "Projekt Work sounds grate!" it said. (Claudia has this little problem with spelling. She says it stifles her creativity to have to spell things the same way every time.) "Meet us by the fense," the note went on. "C U soon!"

I knew that "us" meant Claud and the other members of the BSC, and "by the fense" meant that we were meeting near the fence in the parking lot, which is where we often gather before and after school. Sure enough, when I arrived at the "fense," I found the other members of the BSC already there. Kristy Thomas, carrying a baseball bat, was talking to Logan Bruno, one of our associate members (and the only boy in the club). Logan was holding his girlfriend Mary Anne Spier's hand. Mary Anne was facing away from him, though, talking to Claudia. And Jessi Ramsey and Mallory Pike were chattering away off to the side.

What were they all talking about? Project Work, of course. Everybody was excited about it, and everybody had ideas and dreams about what they might like to do. Jessi and Mal were talking about working at a riding stable (they both love horses), and Kristy and Logan were trying to figure out whether they could play ball at Shea Stadium (they're both big Mets fans). Mary Anne was saying something about running a country inn. And Claudia was talking about working as a guide at the Metropolitan Museum of Art.

"Whoa, hold it!" I said. "These are supposed to be *local* jobs, aren't they?"

"Sure," said Claudia, giggling. "But we can dream, can't we? We're just fooling around."

"Well, in that case," I said, "I think I'd like to be president of the Gap."

Claudia grinned. "Does that mean your best friend will get a discount?" she asked.

Just then, Kristy saw her bus pull up. The rest of us walk home, but Kristy lives across town and takes the bus. "Gotta run!" she said. "I'll see you later. Let's talk about Project Work during the meeting."

We would all be together again in just a few hours, for our Friday BSC meeting: the baseball player, the museum guide, the innkeeper, the stable workers, and the president of a huge clothing chain. What a crew!

CHAPTER 2

"I don't know," mused Claudia. "Maybe it would be more fun to work at the Museum of Modern Art." She and I were in her room, waiting for the other members of the BSC to arrive for our meeting. We were still fantasizing about dream jobs.

"And maybe, instead of the Gap, I'd like to run a really *fancy* clothing business, like Chanel or something," I said. I pictured a fashion show in Paris, with gorgeous models wearing outrageous clothes. "You could design the clothes, Claud, and I'll run the business." I lay back on Claudia's bed and hugged a pillow.

"Sounds awesome," said Claudia.

Just then, Kristy burst into the room. "I've been thinking," she said, without even saying hi. That's Kristy for you. "Project Work probably means we're going to have to make some temporary changes in the BSC," she went on. She plopped down in the director's chair at

Claud's desk, grabbed a pencil, and began to make a list on the back of an envelope. Claudia and I exchanged an amused glance. Kristy is a dynamo. You'll never catch *her* lying around fantasizing. She's a woman of action.

Kristy is our club's president. In fact, the original idea for the BSC was hers. She guessed that parents would love to be able to call one number and reach several responsible sitters — and she was one hundred percent right. Our club now meets in Claudia's room three times a week, on Mondays, Wednesdays, and Fridays from five-thirty to six. Parents can call during those times and set up sitting jobs. And wow, do they call. We always have plenty of work.

Our clients keep coming back because, as Kristy says, "we offer a quality service." Good baby-sitting, that is. We keep on top of our charges' special needs, for one thing. The club notebook helps us with that. That's where we write up every job we go on, so everybody knows what's happening with the kids we sit for. Also, instead of just plopping the kids in front of the TV, the way some sitters do, we have *fun* with them. For example, sometimes we bring along our Kid-Kits, which are boxes packed with hand-me-down toys and games, plus new stickers and crayons and markers. The kids we sit for love to see us arrive with

Kid-Kits in hand. We're also very responsible about scheduling jobs carefully, with the help of our record book, in which we keep track of every member's schedule. We never "stand up" a client.

Kid-Kits, the club notebook, and the record book were all Kristy's ideas. Like I said, she's a dynamo. Kristy is short, with brown hair and brown eyes. She doesn't waste any time on fashion or makeup: her daily "uniform" is a turtleneck shirt, jeans, and running shoes. The running shoes are important, because Kristy's life keeps her on the run. For example, Kristy coaches Kristy's Krushers, a softball team for little kids.

She also has a very busy home life these days. Kristy grew up with two older brothers, Charlie and Sam, and one younger one named David Michael. Kristy's dad skipped out on the family when David Michael was just a baby, and for a long time things weren't easy for the Thomas family. But then Mrs. Thomas met — and eventually married — a really nice guy named Watson Brewer. Watson happens to be rich and, soon after the wedding, the Thomases moved across town to live in his mansion. Along with their new home came more additions to the family. Watson has two kids from his first marriage, Karen and Andrew, who live at the mansion part time. Plus,

Kristy now has a brand-new little sister: Emily Michelle, a Vietnamese girl whom Kristy's mom and Watson adopted. And Kristy's grandmother lives with the family as well. Add in the pets (Shannon, a Bernese Mountain Dog puppy, Boo-Boo the cat, and a couple of goldfish), and you've got one hectic household.

Kristy's best friend is Mary Anne Spier, the secretary of the BSC. Her job is to keep the record book up-to-date. Now, while Kristy goes through life like a hurricane, Mary Anne is more like the eye of the storm. She's quiet and shy and very, very sensitive. Mary Anne is the best listener I know. If you tell her about something that's upset you, her big brown eyes will fill with tears and she'll say just the right thing. And if you're happy, nobody could be happier *for* you than Mary Anne. In a word, Mary Anne is loveable. Maybe that's why she's the only member of the club who has a steady boyfriend. He's Logan Bruno, the associate member, and he's seriously cute and also the sweetest guy at SMS.

That day, a bright-eyed Mary Anne entered Claud's room soon after Kristy started scribbling out her list. "Hey, you guys, guess what?" she said, as she settled into her regular spot on Claud's bed. "I talked to Dawn last night. She's doing great, *and* she says she's

14

really looking forward to coming home in a few months."

Dawn Schafer is Mary Anne's stepsister, and another member of the BSC. She's in California right now, living temporarily with her father and her younger brother, Jeff. Here's how she and Mary Anne became stepsisters: First of all, Mary Anne's mom died when Mary Anne was a baby. Mr. Spier brought Mary Anne up all by himself, and although he was often a little too strict, he basically did a great job. (How else would she be so loveable?) While Mary Anne was growing up in Stoneybrook, Dawn was growing up in California, with her mom, her dad, and Jeff. Then, Dawn's parents got divorced, and Mrs. Schafer brought her kids back to Stoneybrook, which is where *she* had grown up. Dawn and Mary Anne became friends, and soon discovered that their parents had dated when they were in high school. They schemed to get them back together, and the rest is history. Now Mary Anne's dad and Dawn's mom (whom Mary Anne calls Sharon) are husband and wife, and Dawn and Mary Anne are stepsisters, and they live in an old, old farmhouse. Pretty cool, right?

Here's the downside: Before Sharon and Mr. Spier got married, Dawn's brother Jeff realized that he was never going to adjust to life in

Connecticut. He missed California — and his dad — so much that everyone decided it would be best for him to go back and live there. Dawn felt at home in Stoneybrook, but not too long ago she started to miss Jeff and her dad a lot. That's why she's out there now. She went to live with them for awhile, and now *we* miss *her* like crazy. Mary Anne, especially. I could tell she was really happy to hear that Dawn was looking forward to coming back.

Dawn, who has long, long blonde hair and cornflower-blue eyes, is a true individual. She goes her own way, without worrying too much about what the rest of the world is doing. Her job in the BSC (when she's here) is alternate officer, which means she can take over for any other officer who can't attend a meeting. We don't need an alternate officer every day, but there are times when the job is essential.

That's why Shannon Kilbourne, who is usually an associate member like Logan, has temporarily replaced Dawn. Shannon, who has curly blonde hair and a ski-jump nose, lives in Kristy's new neighborhood and goes to a private school. As one of our associate members, she used to be on call to take jobs when we had more than we could handle. Lately, though, she's been acting as a full-fledged member, attending meetings regularly and taking on lots of sitting jobs. (Logan attends meetings only when he wants to.) Shannon has two little sisters, Tiffany and Maria. She's a great student, and she's always involved in after-school activities.

That day she arrived soon after Mary Anne did. "Whew!" she said, eyeing Claud's digital clock. "I just made it, didn't I? I was at a drama club meeting, and my friend's mom drove me here afterward. She isn't familiar with this neighborhood, and she kept making wrong turns even though I thought I was giving her good directions!"

Kristy glanced at the clock. It was 5:28, and I knew she was dying to start the meeting. But I also knew she would wait until exactly 5:30, because that's just the way Kristy is. She's a strong believer in punctuality, to put it mildly.

Claudia groped around under her bed and came up with a bag of Hershey's Miniatures. "I found these last night," she said. "I hid them so well that at first I couldn't remember where they were." Although Claud loves junk food, her parents don't like her to eat it. So she hides it all over her room, along with the Nancy Drew books her parents don't approve of (they think she should be reading "more challenging material"), and pulls it out when we have meetings. She also keeps pretzels and whole-wheat crackers on hand for me. As vice-president of the club, that's one of her only real duties, and it's an unoffical one. Mostly she's the vice-president because the club meets in her room — and we meet in her room because she's the only BSC member with her own phone and a private line. Which reminds me of another one of her duties. Claud handles any BSC calls that come in when we're *not* meeting.

Kristy accepted the bag of candy and started picking out the Special Dark bars. While she poked around, Jessi Ramsey and Mallory Pike rushed into the room.

Jessi and Mal are best friends, and the only junior officers of the club. They're called junior officers because unlike the rest of us, who are thirteen and in the eighth grade, Mal and Jessi are eleven and in sixth. They can't baby-sit at night, except for their own families. Jessi has a younger sister named Becca and a little brother called Squirt. (His real name is John Philip, Jr.). Mal comes from a *huge* family: she has seven younger brothers and sisters! Three of them are identical triplets: Adam, Byron, and Jordan. Then there are Vanessa, Nicky, Margo, and Claire. It's no wonder Mal's such a good sitter.

Jessi is African-American, with coal-dark

eyes, cocoa-colored skin, and the long, limber body of a dancer. She studies ballet very seriously, and may be a ballerina someday. Mal has red hair, glasses, and braces. (They're the clear kind, and don't really show, but she hates them anyway.) Mal is a talented writer and artist, and hopes someday to write and illustrate children's books.

Jessi and Mal had arrived just in time. Right after they got settled on the floor, the clock clicked to 5:30. "Order!" said Kristy. The meeting had begun. "Any new business?" she asked first.

I kept quiet. It was a Friday, which meant I didn't have to collect dues. As treasurer of the club, I do that on Mondays. We all pitch in to help pay Claud's phone bill and Kristy's transportation costs. (Her brother Charlie drives her to meetings.) Nobody loves paying dues, but I have to admit that I like to collect them and keep track of all our money. Maybe someday I'll invest some of it, and surprise everybody by making a killing on the stock market! Or maybe not. Kristy would have a fit.

When nobody answered Kristy, she plowed right ahead. "Well, *I* have some new business," she said. "Project Work is going to change the way we run the club for awhile, from what I can tell. It's a special class at

19

SMS," she explained, turning to Shannon.

Just then, the phone rang and Kristy answered it. It was Mrs. Perkins, one of our regular clients, looking for a sitter for Saturday. The BSC swung into business mode. Mary Anne checked the record book and told us who was free: Jessi, Mary Anne, and Claud. Claud said she had an art project planned, and Mary Anne said she was going shopping with Sharon, so Jessi got the job. Kristy called Mrs. Perkins back, and in minutes everything was all set up.

"Now, where was I?" said Kristy, after she'd hung up. She glanced at the notes she'd made earlier. "Okay, here's the thing. We're all going to be working three days a week after school. The way I see it, we're going to have to cut down our BSC meetings to one a week. Plus, we're going to have to be extra careful about how many sitting jobs we take on."

We glanced at Shannon. She had just gotten used to making time in her schedule for BSC meetings, and now Kristy was telling her that *we* wouldn't have time. Shannon smiled. "It's fine with me," she said. "Maybe I can cover the phone on the days we aren't meeting. But tell me more about Project Work."

We spent the rest of the meeting — between phone calls — talking about Project Work.

Kristy thought it would be a good idea if we all worked at the Washington Mall, just so our schedules would be co-ordinated, and we started talking about which stores and businesses we'd like to work at. Even if only half of them had agreed to accept Project Work kids, there would still be dozens to choose among. The mall is absolutely huge. We weren't fantasizing anymore, but it was almost more exciting to think about what we *really* might be doing. I could hardly wait to get started.

CHAPTER 3

Mr. Withum, my Project Work teacher, was a nice surprise. I'd never had him for a teacher before (he was new at SMS) so I didn't know what to expect. From hearing his name, I had imagined a kind of shriveled, gray-haired man. But he turned out to be "pleasantly plump," as my mother would say, with a big, round pink face and a cheerful smile.

After introducing himself, he explained in more detail how the class would work. All of the Project Work teachers had divided up the available jobs. We would be able to pick from the list he had made, which mostly included jobs in Stoneybrook and at the mall. I listened closely when he explained how, for the six weeks of Project Work, the kids who were working at the mall would be bussed to their jobs on Monday, Tuesday, and Wednesday afternoons. I was just hoping I could find a job I liked at the mall, so I could be on the same schedule as my friends.

"During school we'll meet three times a week," Mr. Withum went on, "to check in with each other and talk about how the jobs are going." Then he handed a stack of job lists to the first person in each row and told them to pass the lists back.

Austin Bentley raised his hand. "What if we get fired from our jobs?" he asked with a grin. "Do we fail the class?" I like Austin, but he can be a wise guy.

Mr. Withum smiled. "This class is unfailable," he said. "*If* you got fired, which I doubt would happen, I'd ask you to write up the experience in your job diary. And then I'd ask you to find another job. It would all be part of learning what it's like to work in the real world."

Kara Mauricio, who was sitting in front of me, handed back the job lists. I took one and passed the rest of them on. Then I scanned the list, hoping I'd see the perfect job right away. There are some great clothing stores at the mall, and I'd been fantasizing about working at one of them. This one called Zingy's has very cool stuff, but I didn't see it on the list. I was disappointed.

The class was buzzing as everybody looked

over the list. "All *right!*" said this guy named Gordon Brown. "Donut Express. That's for me!" Donut Express is a place just outside of Stoneybrook that sells — you guessed it — doughnuts. It's a great place to pig out, even though whenever I go there I have to limit myself to the bagels. "I *love* those chocolate cream-filled ones," Gordon went on. He looked hungry.

"This job at Bellair's looks cool," said Kara. "Women's accessories. I could get into that."

"Dibs on the job at the bike shop!" yelled Austin.

"Okay, hold on just a minute," said Mr. Withum. "Let's do this in an orderly fashion. I'll go down the list, and if I call out a job you want, raise your hand." He started reading out the names of businesses.

Meanwhile, I looked the list over more carefully. Zingy's was out, but there were several other choices at the mall. Then I saw it. "Perfect," I said. Near the bottom of the list was Toy Town, which is a terrific toy store. I've browsed through it plenty of times, looking for little items for my Kid-Kit. Toy Town carries all the regular toys, but it also has some really neat stuff that you can't get everywhere else, such as kits for bug-collecting, or a make-your-own kite package. I guess they're called "educational" toys, but they're not boring.

They're cool. Some of the kids I sit for have found great things at Toy Town. Charlotte Johanssen, my favorite sitting charge, bought a great stuffed dinosaur there.

Just as I was trying to remember what Charlotte had named the dinosaur (I think it was Jasper) I heard Mr. Withum call out, "Anybody for Toy Town?"

My hand shot up. I looked around nervously to see if anybody else wanted to work there, but my hand was the only one raised. Mr. Withum took down my name, and that was it. I had a job!

Once all the jobs were assigned, Mr. Withum told us we'd be visiting our new employers on Wednesday, for orientation, and that our jobs would actually start on the following Monday.

As soon as class was dismissed, I ran to my locker. As I'd hoped, Claud was waiting there for me. "Did you get a job?" she asked eagerly. I nodded.

"At Toy Town," I said.

"All right!"

"What about you?"

"I got the exact one I wanted," she replied. "At the Artist's Exchange."

I squealed and gave her a hug. The Artist's Exchange is this great art supply store where Claudia sometimes buys oil paints and special markers and stuff. "You'll be perfect there," I said. "You know about everything they carry."

"Well, not *everything*," she said. "But I'll learn. This is going to be so cool."

As soon as I finished at my locker, we headed outside. I couldn't wait to find out what jobs everybody else had landed. The other members of the BSC were waiting by the fence, and as Claud and I crossed the parking lot, Kristy caught sight of us. "Did you get jobs at the mall?" she yelled, cupping her hands around her mouth. I gave her the thumbs up sign, and she grinned at me.

When we joined our friends, everybody was talking at once, and at first it was hard to sort out who had gotten which job. "Hey!" yelled Kristy. "Order!"

"Kristy, this isn't a meeting," I said. "You *can't* call us to order."

"Oh, right." Kristy looked a little embarrassed. "I just wanted to hear about everybody's jobs," she explained.

"Me, too," I said. "How about if we take turns telling each other?"

"Great," she said. "As president, I'll go first." We laughed. "I have the coolest job," Kristy said, ignoring us. "Get this — I'm going to be working for mall security!" She swaggered a little. "I'll be on patrol, making sure the mall is crime-free."

Logan gave her a high-five. "Sounds great," he said. "I got a job at Casa Grande's take-out counter in the food court. If we get any banditos over there, I'll know who to call."

"Casa Grande!" said Mal. "That's my favorite place in the whole mall. I love their Super Burritos. I'll be stopping by on my break. I'm going to be working at the BookCenter."

"That's perfect for you, Mal," I said. The BookCenter is a really nice bookstore, with a huge children's section. "I'll be down the hall at Toy Town."

"And I'll be upstairs from you both," said Mary Anne. "At Critters, the pet supply store. It's on the third floor."

"Oh, I know why you picked *that* job," said Kristy. "You just want to scope out all the latest cat toys, for Tigger." Tigger is Mary Anne's kitten. She spoils him rotten.

Mary Anne blushed. "Well, that's kind of true," she said. "But I also thought it would be fun to work at a place where people buy things for their pets. And I'm so glad it's not a regular pet store, with puppies and kittens crammed in those tiny cages."

"I'll be working as an usher at the Cinema

World, way up on the fourth floor," said Jessi. "It wasn't my first choice, but I think it'll be fun. I guess I'll be able to see movies for free, anyway."

Kristy's bus pulled up then, and she had to run for it — but a few hours later we were together again for a BSC meeting in Claud's room, and our discussion continued.

We talked some more about how to run the club during the six weeks of Project Work. We decided to meet once a week, on Fridays. Shannon said she could answer the phone on Mondays and Wednesdays, and take a lot of the early afternoon jobs on Mondays, Tuesdays, and Wednesdays. It looked as if we were all set.

As soon as school ended that Wednesday, I headed for the bus that would take my friends and me to the mall. Kristy had already claimed the two back rows, and I grabbed the seat next to her. "I had to fight Alan Gray for these seats," she said, "but I won."

Alan, who is just about the most obnoxious boy in our class, turned around and crossed his eyes at us. "You'll be sorry," he said. "I'm going to be working at Just Desserts, and I'll put ants on top of your ice cream instead of chocolate sprinkles."

"Yum," said Kristy, giggling. "I love ants."

The ride to the mall was fun, and I realized that spending time on the bus with my friends was going to be great. It was a half hour long each way, plenty of time to catch up with each other and talk about all the stuff we try to gab about during BSC meetings.

When we reached the mall, we scattered. Jessi headed for the elevator, which would take her to Cinema World. Mary Anne stepped onto the escalator and waved to us as she rode up to Critters. Kristy headed for the security offices, walking along with Mal, who was on her way to the BookCenter. Logan loped off toward the food court. Then, Claud walked me to Toy Town, since The Artist's Exchange is right around the corner from it. "Have fun," she said. "If you get done a little early, come get me. Maybe we'll have time to go upstairs and check out Zingy's."

I walked into Toy Town, feeling a little nervous all of a sudden. I was about to meet my new boss! I glanced around at the colorful store, and then I looked down at the card I was carrying, to check my boss's name one last time.

"Well, hello!" I heard a woman say. "You must be Stacey." I looked up to see a tall woman with long, curly red hair, an armful of silver bracelets, and a big smile. She was wearing a white blouse and a swirling purple skirt that looked as if it were made out of silk. And on her hip, she held a little boy with red hair like hers.

"Ms. Frenning?" I asked.

"Please, call me April," she said. "And this is Sandy, my son. Say hi, Sandy." Sandy frowned at me and turned his face away. "He's a little shy sometimes," said April apologetically. "Anyway, welcome to Toy Town. Is this your first time in the store?"

"Oh, no," I said. "I've been here before. I love this store."

"Terrific," said April. "You know what? I can already tell we're going to get along just fine."

April was right. By the end of the afternoon, I felt as if I'd known her forever. She gave me a tour of the store, pointing out the newest and most interesting merchandise. She explained pricing and showed me how to run the cash register. And we even took time out to play with a new item she'd just gotten in — a realistic-looking rubber spider that jumped when you pressed a bulb that was attached to it by a tube. We made it leap all over the store, and soon we were laughing so hard we were practically crying.

Sandy, on the other hand, actually *was* crying, at least some of the time. April explained that he was bored, since she had been having trouble finding child care for him lately and he'd had to spend a lot of time with her at the store. But even though he was a little cranky, I could tell Sandy was a great kid.

"I'm looking forward to having you here on Monday," April said, when it was time for me to head for the bus. "I think we're going to have fun."

I was sure she was right. I could hardly wait to start my new job.

CHAPTER 4

Slinkys. Dinosaur puzzles, farm puzzles, zoo puzzles, puzzles of every description. Cowboy hats and ballerina tiaras. Stuffed bears, stuffed rabbits, and stuffed whales. Train sets, doctor kits, puppets . . . there was so much to look at in Toy Town! When I arrived there on Monday for my first real day of work, April told me to take some time to explore the store and get familiar with the merchandise. I walked up and down the aisles, amazed at how much could be packed into one small store. The week before, when April had showed me around, I had been too excited and nervous to take everything in. But now, I was paying more attention.

The place was like heaven for little kids. I pictured myself at eight or nine years old. At that age, I could have happily spent all my time in a place like Toy Town. And it wasn't just the toys. April had made the store into a very welcoming place. There were display tables, for example, where toys were set out for kids to look at and play with. One of them held a train set, with trees and buildings and even a lake made out of a mirror. On the other was a farm scene, with horses and cows and pigs and sheep all spilling out of a big red barn. I picked up a horse to look it over more closely.

"Mine!" said Sandy from behind me. He was frowning, and he held out his hand for the horse.

"Unfortunately, Sandy thinks everything in the store belongs to him," said April, scooping him up. She hugged Sandy and kissed the top of his head. "Makes it difficult to sell things sometimes."

"Two-year-olds can be that way," I said. " 'Mine' is their favorite word, isn't it? I babysit a lot, so I'm used to it." I told April a little about the BSC.

"What a great idea," said April. "I could sure use a BSC in my neighborhood!"

"So," I said, eager to start working, "what would you like me to do today?"

"Let's see," said April. "I've been thinking about changing the display tables. Why don't you put away the farm and set up this dollhouse in its place?" She showed me a carton containing a snap-together dollhouse, and a few other boxes that held furniture and brightly colored plastic people. "The farm stuff goes in these," she said, handing me some empty boxes. "After you've done that, you can take your break, and then maybe I can give you another lesson on the cash register. Does that sound okay?"

"It sounds great," I said. I got down on my knees and started to take the barn apart. I didn't really feel I would *need* a break that afternoon, but all the Project Work jobs followed the same schedule. Mr. Withum had told us about it that day in class. "You'll work for two hours every afternoon," he had said, "with a fifteen-minute break at some point. Please be sure you're on time, and don't abuse your break privileges." My friends and I had already planned to visit each other on our breaks.

I was busy separating the animals into various piles when April returned. "By the way," she said. "I forgot to mention one important thing. While you're in the store, I'd like you to keep an eye out for shoplifters. Merchandise walks out of this store all the time, especially the little things up front near the cash register."

"That's awful," I said.

April shrugged. "It's a fact of life," she said. "All stores have to deal with it. Lately, though, it seems as if it's happening more than ever." She looked over at Sandy, who was tearing into a pile of puzzles. "Oh, no, Sandy!" she said, running to stop him.

"He can help me," I said, "if you want to keep him busy, that is."

"That would be great," said April. "Sandy, want to help Stacey with the farm?" she asked.

"Hoss!" said Sandy, pointing at the horse I held in my right hand.

"Good!" I said. "Can you find the right pile for the horsie?" I handed it to him. Sandy and I spent a peaceful half hour packing up the farm animals. Then, just as I was pulling the dollhouse pieces out of their boxes, Claudia turned up.

"You look like *you're* having a good time," she said. "What a great job. You get to play all day!"

"How's *your* job?" I asked.

"It's the coolest," said Claud. "You wouldn't believe how much I've learned in one day! They have these amazing new acrylic paints over there. I've already decided to save up for them."

"You're going to become their best customer," I said, smiling.

"I know," she admitted. "But I don't mind spending my money there. The owners are really nice people." She frowned. "I can't believe anybody would steal stuff from them, but they said they have a problem with shoplifting. It's been much worse lately."

"April said the same thing about Toy Town," I said. "It's a shame."

Claudia picked up the mother doll from the pile on the table. "I wish I'd had a dollhouse like this when I was little," she said, checking out the mother's tiny plastic shoes.

"Mine," said Sandy.

"Oh," I said. "I forgot to introduce you to Sandy. He's April's son."

"Nice to meet you," said Claudia, bending down to say hi to him. She handed him the doll. "And now I've got to run. My break's almost up."

"See you on the bus!" I said.

I spent the next half hour putting together the dollhouse. Sandy helped, and we had a great time. Just as I was setting the dollhouse father in the kitchen and the mother in the garage (this was a liberated doll family, I had decided), April came over to take a look. "Wonderful," she said. "Why don't you go ahead and take your break?" She picked up Sandy. "And you, young man, can help me at the cash register."

I left the store and decided to head down the hall to see Mal at the bookstore. I found her in the children's section, of course. She was arranging books on the shelves. "Stacey!" she said, when she saw me. "Isn't this the coolest store? I *love* it here. Look at this book that just came in. Aren't the illustrations fantastic?"

Mal's face was flushed. I was glad to see her so happy. A bookstore really is the perfect place for her. I looked at the book she handed me, which was an updated version of *Little Red Riding Hood*. "Cool," I said. "I can see *you* making a book like this someday."

"That would be awesome," said Mal. "Can you imagine going to a bookstore and seeing books with your name on them?"

A woman walked by just then, and smiled at Mal. "Whoa!" said Mal. "That's Ms. Munro, my manager. She's really nice, but she probably wants me to get back to work." Mal watched as the woman moved away. "She walks around the store like that all day, watching for shoplifters," she added. "Apparently it's kind of a problem here. And Jessi stopped by before and told me that her bosses at Cinema World are upset because people are always trying to sneak into the movies."

I handed the book back to Mal. "It's awful," I said. "Until I worked here, I didn't know there was so much of that kind of thing going on at the mall. But it happens at Claud's store, and at Toy Town, too." We looked at each other and shrugged. "Well, see you later!" I said. "I'll let you get back to work. I'm going to head upstairs to see Mary Anne."

At Critters, Mary Anne was working on a window display. She held up a dog toy shaped like a hamburger. "Don't you think this would look good near that other one, the one that looks like a hot dog?" she asked. She squeezed the toy and it squeaked. We giggled.

"Hey, Mary Anne," I said, suddenly curious. "Do people ever steal stuff like that from here?"

"Funny you should ask," she said. "That was one of the first things the store owner told me to look out for. I didn't really believe him, but I guess it's true. Personally, I can't imagine a dog- or cat-lover stealing anything, but according to him, it happens all the time."

I shook my head, frowning.

"Not only that," Mary Anne added, "but Logan stopped by here on his break, and guess what he told me? There's even shoplifting going on at the food court."

I raised my eyebrows. Mary Anne nodded. "It's true," she said. "People walk off with pretzels and stuff while the workers are busy getting the rest of their orders."

"Speaking of busy," I said, glancing at my watch, "I'd better get back to Toy Town. My break's just about over." I said good-bye to

Mary Anne and headed for the escalator.

"Hey, Stacey!" I turned to see Kristy walking toward me. She was wearing a black baseball cap that said "Washington Mall Security" in gold script, and a walkie-talkie hung from her belt.

"Hey, Officer Thomas," I replied. "Enjoying your job?" We stepped onto the escalator together.

She grinned. "It's great."

"I hear there's a lot of shoplifting going on around here," I said.

"That's right. But we're on the case." Her walkie-talkie made a crackling noise, and she grabbed it just as we reached the bottom of the escalator.

"I have to run," I said. "I'm going to be late."

Kristy nodded as she put the walkie-talkie to her ear. "See you on the bus," she said.

Back at Toy Town, April was busy at the cash register, and a line of people was waiting to be helped. "What can I do?" I asked.

April nodded toward the back of the store, where a boy was playing noisily near the train set. "Encourage him to use the display toys," she said. "I try to leave enough out, but the kids always go for the new stuff."

I walked back and discovered that the boy, who looked about seven, was tearing into a

39

new package of Legos. Another package, already opened, was at his feet. "How about leaving those on the shelf?" I said. "We can check out this train set instead."

He just stared at me.

I looked around for his mother. "Where's your mom?" I asked. "Or are you here with your dad? Or a baby-sitter?"

"My mom's shopping," the boy answered. "She said she'd be back soon."

I couldn't believe it. This boy's mother had left him here, all by himself! I spent a few minutes helping him clean up the Legos, and by the time we finished, his mother had turned up. "Have a good time, Jason?" she asked. She turned to me. "I always leave him here while I shop. He's happier, and I can be a lot more productive."

I watched her leave, shaking my head. April saw me and smiled. "I know, it's awful," she said. "But it happens all the time, and what can I do? It's not like there's any better place to leave a kid while you shop." She shrugged. I was amazed she took it so well. The idea seemed crazy to me.

On the way home that afternoon, my friends and I talked about our first day on the job. I told my friends about Jason's mom leaving him at the store, and to my surprise they were not shocked. Mal had heard about the same thing happening at the bookstore, and Logan had seen kids left at the food court.

I've always liked Washington Mall, and I loved my new job, but I was beginning to wonder about a few things. Shoplifting, kids left alone. Working in the real world was an eye-opener.

JOB DIARY . . . . Mallory Pike

    When Ms. Munro, the manager at
the Book Center, asked me if I'd
like to run a story hour for kids,
I jumped at the chance. I've never
done a story hour before, but I knew
it would be fun. After all, I love
books and I love kids. What could
be so hard about it? Well, today I
found out....

Mal's job at the BookCenter was going well. Her manager was friendly and helpful, the work wasn't too hard, and Mal adored being surrounded by books. She especially loved the children's section and Ms. Munro let her work there most afternoons. The BookCenter has the best selection of children's books Mal had ever seen in a bookstore. On top of that, the area is set up to make kids feel at home. There are pillows to lounge on, small, child-sized chairs, and stuffed animals scattered around. Kids who come into the store are encouraged to check out the books on the shelves, and sit down for a closer look at the ones that interest them.

Plus, the children's section has a small "stage" area for puppet shows, storytellers, and story hour.

"We haven't had a story hour in about a month," Ms. Munro had told Mal the week before. "One of our staff members took some time off because she had a baby. But I have a feeling you'd be great at it."

And that was how Mal was talked into story hour. It didn't take much persuading, because Mal thought it sounded like fun. But when she arrived at the store that afternoon and saw the big sign outside advertising story hour — with *her* name, Mallory Pike, in bold red letters

— well, that's when she started to feel nervous. Maybe, she thought, this was a bigger deal than she had realized.

She headed for the children's section and found Ms. Munro there, setting up the stage. There was a chair for Mal, with a pile of books next to it. "I hope you don't mind, but I picked out a few books for your first time," said Ms. Munro. "The kids always like these, and sometimes it's best to start with books that are tried and true. Next time, you can pick out your own."

Mal sat down and looked over the books. One of them was *Stone Soup*, which had been a favorite of her brother Nicky's. Then there was *The Cat in the Hat*, which her sisters Claire and Margo absolutely loved. And the third one was a huge, oversized edition of *Tikki Tikki Tembo*, a book Mal herself had always liked. "These look great," she told Ms. Munro.

"I wish I had more of the really big books," said Ms. Munro, gesturing toward *Tikki Tikki Tembo*. "The kids adore them. Anyway, why don't you take some time to read through those?" She checked her watch. "You have fifteen minutes or so."

But about five minutes later, the kids began to arrive, and before Mal knew it she had what looked to her like a huge audience. "There were probably only fifteen kids there," she told me later, "but from up on the stage it looked like there were fifteen *hundred*."

The kids, who mostly ranged in age from three to five or so, seemed restless. A few parents were there, but a lot of the kids were on their own. Mal figured their parents must be using story hour as sort of a baby-sitter while they went shopping in the mall. The noise level was high as the kids settled in. A boy in the front row was poking his friend, who squealed and giggled and poked him back. Two girls were running from spot to spot, trying to find the best seats. And a baby who sat on its mother's lap was beginning to get fussy. Mal glanced at the clock on the wall. She wasn't supposed to start for another five minutes, but she had a feeling she might have a small riot on her hands if she waited that long.

Taking a deep breath, Mal reached for *Stone Soup*. "Hi," she said, looking out at the crowd of kids. They ignored her. "Hi," she said more loudly. This time they looked up at her. "Welcome to the BookCenter story hour!" she said, trying to sound enthusiastic and confident. "My name is Mallory, and I'm going to read you a few books today."

"Can you read *The Little Red Hen*?" called a

small girl with a red bow in her hair.

"Um, well, not today," said Mal. "Maybe next week."

"How about *Barney and the Bully*?" asked a boy wearing a Barney T-shirt.

Mal didn't even know if such a book existed, so she just shook her head. "I don't have that one, but I think you'll like the ones I *do* have." She held up *Stone Soup*. "This one is called *Stone Soup*. Do any of you know this story?"

A girl in the front row raised her hand. "My teacher read that to us last week," she said. "It's fun."

"Great," said Mal. "Let's get started." She opened the book and began to read.

Do you know the story of *Stone Soup*? There are a few different versions of it, but basically, it's about how a group of people cooperate to make a wonderful meal, even when they think they have no food at all. They start a pot of water boiling, and add some "magic" stones. Then one person adds a carrot, and another one adds a potato, and somebody else adds some cabbage. Before you know it, there's a big pot of delicious soup. It's a great story.

But Mal was having some trouble convincing the *kids* of that fact. They still seemed restless, and they weren't paying much attention. Mal tried to put a lot of expression into her reading, and after she read each page, she held

46

up the book so the kids could see the picture. She even tried to read with the book held up next to her, so they could see the picture as she read, but that was pretty hard.

Finally one of the boys yelled out, "This is a dumb story. And the pictures are too little. I can't even see what the people look like!"

Mal blushed. Her first story hour was bombing in a big way. She glanced down at the floor and saw *Tikki Tikki Tembo*. "Okay," she said. "How about if we move on to the next book? This one has really big pictures." She picked it up and showed it to them.

"Yea!" yelled a couple of kids. Mal looked around at her audience and noticed that it had grown. A couple of slightly older kids were there now, kids Mal thought she had seen in the bookstore before. One was a blonde girl who looked about six, and the other was a boy, obviously her brother (he had the same turned-up nose, Mal told me), and apparently a couple of years older. They were on their own, and they were a little dirty and scruffy, but they were behaving well. The girl looked up at Mal and smiled. "I love that book. I can say Tikki Tikki Tembo's whole name," she said.

"Good," said Mal. "I hope everybody will be able to do that by the time we finish reading this." She opened the book and tried to hold it up so everybody could see. It was a *huge* book, so the pictures were big enough, but it was floppy. Mal struggled to keep it upright as she began to read.

Tikki Tikki Tembo is the story of two young brothers who live in a small mountain village in China. One of them is named Chang. He is the second-born son, and so, because it's the custom, he has a very short name. But his older brother, the first-born son, has a long, *long* name and that's what causes the trouble. What happens first is that Chang falls into a well. His brother runs for help, and help comes quickly. But then the older brother, the first born son, falls into the well. And when Chang runs for help, it takes a lot longer. Why? Because every time Chang tries to tell somebody that his brother has fallen into the well, he has to start by saying his brother's name, which is this: Tikki tikki tembo-no sa rembo-chari bari ruchi-pip peri pembo!

Kids, naturally, *love* that book. The name is repeated over and over, and soon they learn to chant it along with whoever is reading to them. By the middle of the story, Mal's arms were tired from holding up the giant book and turning the pages, and her neck was stiff from looking at the book sideways, and her throat was scratchy from reading out loud — but Mal was happy. The kids were crazy about the book, and every time Mal started to say "Tikki tikki tembo," the kids joined in and said it along with her, shouting out the last "pip peri pembo!" so loudly that shoppers from all over the store came to see what was going on in the children's section. Mal was a big hit.

After she finished *Tikki Tikki Tembo*, Mal swung right into *The Cat in the Hat*, which was also a crowd-pleaser. And when Mal finished that, they begged for another. "Sorry," said Mal, who had noticed that a lot of parents were already waiting to pick up their kids. "That's all for today, but come back next week."

By the time Mal had tidied up the children's section, all of the kids had been picked up. The blonde girl and boy were met by an older girl, maybe twelve, Mal thought. She looked as if she might be their sister.

After being congratulated by Ms. Munro, Mal headed for the bus, and we all rode home together. She filled us in on her story hour. "That sounds like fun," said Jessi, enviously. "All I got to do today was sweep up popcorn and scrape chewing gum off the theatre floor."

"I had a good day," said Logan. "The cook at Casa Grande taught me how to make enchiladas."

"Cool," said Claudia. "I had fun today, too. I unpacked a new shipment of paints and set them up in a window display."

"Well, I made my first big sale today," said Mary Anne. "Twenty pounds of dog biscuits to a lady who owns a Saint Bernard."

Then it was my turn to report on that day's work. "My day wasn't so great," I said. "You know all that stuff we heard about shoplifting? Well, it happened to me today. I was right there, too, working at the cash register. Some sing-along cassettes disappeared from practically right under my nose."

"Oh," said Claudia. "That's awful. Was your boss mad?"

"No, she was really nice about it. But still, I feel responsible. I just wish there was something I could do about it."

"I'll look into it," said Kristy importantly. "Security has cameras in every store, you know. I'll make sure my boss reviews today's tapes from Toy Town extra carefully."

"Thanks," I replied. But I didn't hold out much hope that the shoplifters would be caught that way. They had done their job well, and it was my guess that they knew all about the cameras and how to avoid them.

"Speaking of cameras," said Mal, "I wish we'd had one at story hour today. I thought I saw something weird happen, but now I'm not so sure." She told us about the blonde boy and girl, and said that at one point during *Tikki Tikki Tembo* she *thought* she saw the boy pick up and gobble down a pack of cookies that belonged to a little girl sitting nearby. It wasn't a big deal and the girl didn't make a fuss, so Mal thought maybe she'd been mistaken. Still, it bothered her.

"Ooh," said Kristy, grinning. "Crime wave at story hour. What will it be next? Crayon snatching? Puppet kidnapping?"

We cracked up, and I forgot about the bad parts of the day as we talked and laughed for the rest of the ride home.

CHAPTER 6

"So, I talked to my boss some more about the videotapes from Toy Town — " Kristy stopped in mid-sentence and whirled around in her seat. "Alan Gray, you cut that out," she yelled. "Spitballs are disgusting and juvenile. You are *so* immature." Then she raised her hand to her cheek, where another spitball had just landed. *"Alan,"* she said. "We're *trying* to have a serious discussion here!"

It was Monday, and my friends and I were on the bus together, heading to the mall to start our second week of work. I was looking forward to my day at Toy Town, although I was having a hard time forgetting about those cassettes that had disappeared. I had even talked to my mom about it. She told me that there's shoplifting at *every* store, including Bellairs, and that I shouldn't feel guilty that it had happened to me. But I did anyway. April hadn't seemed *too* upset (I guess she was used to it), but it sure bothered me. "So what did she say?" I asked Kristy. She had told us at Friday's BSC meeting that her boss, Ms. Garcia, had planned to review the tapes, but that was the last I had heard.

"Well, she called me on Saturday," said Kristy. "And it turns out that there *were* some people doing suspicious-looking things on the tape. Teenagers — older ones. I guess security has been watching them for a while: they think a gang of kids is responsible for a lot of the shoplifting that's been going on recently."

"Wow!" I said. "A gang? That sounds major."

"Do they have guns and stuff?" asked Mary Anne, looking scared.

"I don't think it's a *gang* gang," said Kristy. "It's just a group of kids out for kicks. But Ms. Garcia is taking them seriously."

"Good," said Claudia. "They shouldn't be allowed to get away with what they're doing. My boss said shoplifting costs him thousands of dollars a year! He said his prices would be a lot lower if he didn't have to make up for what he loses when people shoplift."

"That's what my boss said, too," said Logan.

The bus pulled up at the mall entrance, and we all hopped out. As she passed Alan Gray, Kristy stuck her tongue out and made a face.

"Very mature," I whispered to her. She giggled.

"Have fun, everybody!" she said, as she headed for the security office.

Claud and I walked together until we reached Toy Town. We glanced into store windows as we went by them, checking out new displays of shoes and dresses. "One of these days we're going to have to stay a little late and do some serious shopping," said Claud, eyeing a white lace baby-doll dress. "I'll ask my dad if he can pick us up one day next week."

"Great," I said. "I could use a new pair of shoes." I had hardly thought about shopping, even though I had been spending so much time in the mall. Being there as an employee was very different. Somehow the stores didn't seem to have the same magic, now that I knew what it was like behind the scenes. April had explained a little more about pricing to me, and she'd told me how displays can be used to "move" merchandise that might otherwise sit on the shelves. Still, even though the magic wasn't there anymore, shopping with Claudia was always fun. And knowing more about how stores worked would only make me a better shopper. I gazed at a pair of black lace-up boots and wondered how they would look with this old-fashioned floral-print dress my mother had given me.

"Hey, we're going to be late," said Claud, pulling on my arm.

I checked my watch. "You're right!" I cried. "I better run. See you!" I took off for Toy Town, and arrived a little out of breath.

"Tay-see!" said Sandy, when he saw me walk in the door. He ran to me, grinning. Sandy had turned out to be pretty friendly, and he seemed to like me a lot, maybe because April kept asking me to play with him whenever he started to get cranky and bored. "See my doggie?" Sandy asked, holding up a black-and-white stuffed puppy. "Ruff, ruff," he said, giggling as he made the dog jump up and down.

"You can show Stacey your doggie later, honey," said April, stepping out from behind the cash register. "Right now, Stacey and I need to have a little talk, so I want you to sit quietly for a few minutes, okay?"

Sandy nodded, and April settled him into a corner with his dog and a little blanket made out of a towel. "You tuck your doggie in, and tell him a bedtime story," she said.

Then she turned to me. I was just standing there, shifting my weight from side to side and feeling extremely nervous. What did she want to talk to me about? Was she going to tell me I couldn't work at Toy Town anymore? Had she decided that it was my fault, after all, that those cassettes had disappeared?

"I need to talk to you about shoplifting," said April. "Why don't we sit down for a few minutes?" She gestured toward a pair of kid-sized chairs standing next to the train-set table.

A knot had formed in my stomach, and as I walked toward the chair I felt it growing. "I'm really sorry about what happened on Wednesday," I said as soon as we sat down. "I'll pay you back for the cassettes, if you want."

"Oh, Stacey," said April, reaching out to touch my arm. "That's not what I wanted to talk to you about. That wasn't your fault at all!" She smiled at me. "You're a wonderful worker, and I trust you completely."

"Thanks," I said, relieved.

"I just wanted to go over some procedures with you. Security came around and talked to all the store owners last Friday. They're concerned about the major increase in shoplifting lately, and they want us to be on the lookout. Also, they asked us to talk to our staffs about what to do if they see someone stealing something." She held up her hand and started to count off on her fingers. "First of all," she said, "keep your eyes peeled for people who linger in the store without buying anything. People who are carrying big bags or wearing oversized coats or jackets are suspicious, too. Watch them if they make a move toward merchandise. But if you see somebody take something, don't go after the person yourself, whatever you do. That could be dangerous. Next, don't panic. And don't make it obvious that you saw them. Instead, you should press our security button, which will alert security to a problem at Toy Town, and they'll get here as fast as they can."

"Where's the button?" I asked. I had never seen April so serious, and the discussion was making me nervous.

"It's under the counter, right below the cash register," said April. "I'll show you." She stood up, and I followed her to the counter. Sure enough, a little red button was hidden underneath. "Nobody can tell if you press it," she said. "And it definitely works. Security re-tested all the buttons over the weekend."

"Mommy!" cried Sandy, running to us. "Doggie woke up!"

"Okay, Sandy," said April, patting his head. "Want to come help Mommy unpack some boxes?" She looked at me and smiled. "I hope I didn't scare you, Stacey, but this is important stuff. Anyway, I have to unload some new merchandise now. Can you work the counter for awhile?"

"Sure," I said. I tried to sound confident, even though I was feeling pretty shaky. I would have preferred to unpack boxes with Sandy, but I didn't want April to know I was scared. I watched her head for the back room, and then I turned my attention to the counter. I tidied up a display of troll key rings and re-filled a box of miniature yo-yo's. I checked the batteries on the display sample of a Gamester, a hand-held computer game. Then a man and a woman walked into the store as I was straightening up a bunch of pinwheels. I checked the couple out. The woman was wearing a long coat, and carrying a shopping bag. The man was dressed in a business suit, but a leather backpack was slung over his shoulder. Shoplifters? I had no way of knowing. I moved behind the counter and ran my hand beneath it, checking for the button. The woman had picked up a special microphone that adds sound effects when you talk into it, and I wondered what I would do if she slipped it into her bag.

I ran over April's directions in my mind. "Don't let her know you saw her. Don't chase her. Push the button." It all sounded simple, but what if there were complications? What if a shoplifter were armed? What if he or she were caught and figured out who had fingered him? What would he do to me? My palms felt sweaty, and my heart was beating fast. About five minutes later, though, the couple left. I had watched them closely the whole time, and I was almost positive they hadn't taken anything.

April emerged from the back of the store, brushing her hands off. "Everything okay out here?" she asked.

"Just fine," I said, trying to smile.

"Tay-see!" shouted Sandy, waving his stuffed dog at me. "Play with me!"

April smiled at me. "Could you?" she asked. "I'll be checking the shelves, to see if we need to re-stock anything. You two can play right up front here, and you can run the cash register if we have customers."

"Okay," I said. I was glad to have the distraction of playing with Sandy. I could still keep an eye out for shoplifters, but maybe I wouldn't be quite so nervous. "Let's see your dog," I said to Sandy. "What does a doggie say?"

For the rest of the afternoon, I was so busy I forgot to be nervous. I still checked out every customer who came into the store, but I stopped worrying about whether he might be armed and dangerous. Sandy kept demanding my attention, but I was able to keep him entertained and also watch the store.

Or so I thought. Unfortunately, I was wrong.

As I was getting ready to leave, April approached me with a worried look on her face. "Stacey, have you seen the Gamester?" she asked. "Or did you sell it to someone?"

I shook my head. "I didn't sell it. And the last I saw, it was right there, on the — " I looked at the counter, where the Gamester had been. It was gone.

"I didn't sell it either," said April. "It must have walked out of here." She shook her head. "Darn," she said. "I guess I'll have to report it to security. I'll see you tomorrow, Stacey — and don't worry. It wasn't your fault."

I felt awful. I knew I had watched as well as I could, considering that I was entertaining Sandy and all. But obviously I hadn't watched closely enough.

On the bus going home, I told my friends what had happened.

"That's terrible!" said Kristy. "Those shoplifters must be really good." She banged her fist into her palm.

"Still, I might have caught them, if I hadn't been taking care of Sandy, too," I said. Then, suddenly, I had an amazing idea. "Hey!" I exclaimed. "You know what the mall needs? A day-care center."

"Definitely!" said Claudia. "What a great idea! It could be near the middle of the mall, like the food court, and it could be for shoppers *and* for store-owners like April."

My friends and I spent the rest of our ride talking excitedly about my idea. I was happy to think about something positive, instead of being preoccupied with the disappearance of the Gamester. A day-care center might not solve the shoplifting problem, but it would sure help with a lot of other problems in the mall. And if the members of the BSC put their minds to it, I knew we could make it happen.

C H A P T E R 7

You know how I said all my friends were enthusiastic about my idea for the day-care center? Well, that wasn't totally true. There was one exception: Kristy. I noticed she was a little quieter than usual during the bus ride that afternoon, and she didn't seem so eager to talk about the idea. I wasn't sure why. Maybe she was preoccupied with the shoplifting problem. Maybe she was just tired. Or maybe she was having a hard time accepting the fact that I had come up with a great idea — one she wished *she* had thought of! Kristy's used to being the idea person, and I think it's hard for her sometimes when somebody else comes up with one.

Anyway, by the time we climbed into the bus on Tuesday afternoon, Kristy had recovered from whatever was wrong. She had obviously given the day-care idea a lot of thought overnight, and she couldn't wait to talk about the details. As soon as we found seats on the bus, Kristy whipped out a little notebook and a pen. "Okay," she said. "This day-care center will be great, but there are a lot of aspects we need to figure out."

Claud, who was sitting next to me, nudged me with her elbow and grinned at me. I smiled back. We're used to the way Kristy takes an idea and runs with it.

"First of all," said Kristy, "I can't see why the people at the mall wouldn't go for it. I mean, it's perfect. I'm sure business would increase if people had a place to leave their kids while they shopped. And it'll be great for employees at the stores, too. But where would the center be? And who would pay the rent for it? And who would run it?"

"There's a huge empty storefront over by the games arcade," said Logan. "It would be ideal. And I bet the store-owners would chip in for the rent — or maybe they could work out a deal with the mall management."

"There must be a lot of other store-owners like April, who are parents, too. I bet we could organize a group of them to run the place," I said.

"What about equipment?" asked Mary Anne. "You know, toys and stuff. And mats for naptime."

"Naptime!" said Jessi. "That reminds me.

You know what's strange? My manager told me he thinks somebody's been sleeping overnight in the movie theatre!"

"Weird," I said. It *was* weird, but I was too busy thinking about the day-care idea to pay much attention to what Jessi had said. Instead, I turned to Kristy and said, "We'll need art supplies and books, too."

"Good point," said Kristy, making a note. "Maybe we could get people to donate a lot of these things."

"We could have a fund-raising drive," added Jessi. "For start-up costs."

"I guess the first thing to do is for us to talk to our bosses," I said. "We can see if they think it's a good idea, too. Maybe they'll have some thoughts about what to do next."

And that's how we left it. When the bus pulled up to the mall, we piled out, eager to start on our new project.

But as it turned out, I didn't get a chance to talk to April — not right away, anyway. When I walked into the store, I found her looking frazzled. "Oh, Stacey," she said. "Boy, am I glad to see you. I've been so busy here today that I haven't had a break in hours. Could you run the register for a while? I'll be in the back."

"Sure," I said. I looked over at the counter and noticed that another Gamester was on display. April saw me looking at it.

"I know, I know," she said. "It's tempting fate. But it won't sell if it's not on display, so I'm stuck leaving it out."

"I'll keep an eye on it," I said. I realized that might be easier today, since Sandy didn't seem to be around. "Where's Sandy today?"

"I'm trying out a new sitter," said April. "But she's only available on Tuesdays and Thursdays, so it's not really the ideal solution."

"I wanted to talk to you about that — " I began, but just then a young boy and his mother came up to us and asked about video game cartridges.

"I'll let you handle this," said April, heading for the back of the store. "Call me if you need me."

I showed the boy where the cartridges are displayed, and then headed back to the counter. On my way, I stopped to straighten up a display of rubber stamps. I was putting the last one in its place when I heard a loud commotion just outside the store. I ran to the doorway to look out, and had to jump out of the way as two police officers — a man and a woman — ran by me. I looked past them and saw a bunch of people running down the middle of the mall, past the benches, the main escalator, and the big white marble fountain.

"What's going on?" I asked a woman who was running by.

"Don't know!" she shouted over her shoulder, still running.

People were converging on a spot near the store that sells giant cookies — three doors down from Toy Town — and the whole mall seemed to be watching to see what was happening. Store-owners were peering out through their windows, or standing in their doorways. On the upper levels, people were leaning over the balconies to watch the action. Shoppers walked quickly or ran toward the growing crowd. "Hey!" I heard an older man cry, as somebody knocked into him. The next thing I knew, he was sprawled on the floor, trying to get up. I wanted to help him, but I couldn't leave the store.

I yelled for April, and she came running. By then, several people had stopped to help the man. "What's going on?" asked April. She looked out at the crowd. "What's happening?"

"I can't figure it out," I said.

Just then, I heard shouting, and I saw two teenaged boys break away from the crowd. They started to run in my direction, but the woman police officer chased after them and grabbed them. "You're under arrest," I heard her say loudly. "You have the right to remain silent — "

I turned to April. "Wow!" I said. "I bet they caught the shoplifters."

We looked back at the crowd, and saw that the police seemed to be arresting another boy — a tall guy, with black hair — and two girls. Several security officers were on hand, surrounding the kids. "They must have gotten the whole gang!" I exclaimed. I looked at the boy more closely, and realized I had seen him in the store when I first came in.

Something made me turn from the doorway and glance over at the counter. "The Gamester!" I said. "It's missing!"

"Go tell the police!" said April. "Those kids must have just taken it."

I ran to the crowd, and straight to the woman officer, who was writing something in a little notebook. "I work at Toy Town," I said, out of breath. "We're missing a computer toy. It disappeared within the last few minutes."

She nodded, but didn't speak. Instead, she turned to the cluster of teens who had been arrested and asked them to empty their pockets. One of the girls pulled out an expensive-looking lipstick, and another had hidden a scarf under her jacket. The policewoman told them to drop the stuff on the floor in front of them. Then she glared at the three boys, who hadn't moved yet. "You, too," she said. One of the boys, the one I had seen in the store earlier, started backing away. A security officer took a step toward him, and he shrugged and pulled something out of his pocket.

"The Gamester!" I said out loud. I watched as the guy handed it to the policewoman.

"That's from our store!" I said. "Can I take it back there?"

The boy scowled at me.

The policewoman turned to me and shook her head. "Sorry, but you can't. We'll have to keep it for evidence."

I was disappointed. As soon as I had seen it emerge from the boy's pocket, I had started to imagine how good it would feel to walk back to Toy Town and hand the Gamester to April.

Mal turned up just then. "This is wild," she said. "I can't believe they caught the shop-lifters!"

Kristy, came up behind us, looking awfully happy — and proud. "It was a sting opera-tion," she explained in a whisper. "The whole thing was planned down to the last detail."

"You *knew* about it?" I asked.

"Well, not until I got here today," she ad-mitted. "But I was working as back-up when they made the bust." She was trying to act cool, but suddenly she dropped the act and grinned. "It was *awesome*," she said.

"Does this mean the shoplifting is going to stop now?" Mal asked.

"Absolutely," said Kristy. "You can go back to work and breathe easier."

Mal looked relieved — and I felt as if a weight had dropped off my shoulders. Working at Toy Town would be a real pleasure if I didn't have to worry so much about shoplifters.

When I returned to the store, April was talking to a policeman. "That's wonderful," she said, when he explained that they thought they had caught the entire gang.

The officer left, after handing April a sheaf of police reports to fill out, and we looked at each other and smiled. "That's a load off my mind," said April. "I was actually a little worried sometimes about having Sandy in the store. I mean, what if he got in the way of someone who was armed, and he hurt him?"

"That reminds me," I said. "Remember I said I wanted to talk to you about something?" I explained my idea for the day-care center, and added some of the details my friends and I had come up with that day on the bus.

"That sounds terrific! You girls will need lots of help for a big project like that, but I can already think of four or five store-owners who would love to be involved," said April, smiling. Then her face fell. "The only thing is, you'll need permission from the mall manager, and I don't know if he'll agree."

"Don't you think he'll like the idea?" I asked.

"I don't know. We used to bring up ideas like this with the old manager, Ms. Richards, and she never went for them. But now that there's a new guy on the job — well, you never know. I guess it's worth trying. You and your friends might have better luck."

"There's a new manager?" I asked.

April nodded. "He's been working here for about six months," she said. She picked up the police reports and began to look them over.

I wanted to ask her a few more questions — such as how she thought we should approach the manager — but she looked busy, and anyway it was time to catch my bus home.

I left the mall that day feeling hopeful. The shoplifters had been caught, and now we might have a chance to start working on our day-care center. Things were looking up.

CHAPTER 8

JOB DIARY . . . . Kristy Thomas

Everybody at the mall seems to think a day care center would be a good idea. My boss, Ms. Garcia, thinks so. So does my friend Stacey's boss, April Frenning. She's planning to be very involved in running the place, and she's already talked to a couple of other mall employees who want to help, too. And the managers at the movie theatre, the pet supply store, the Book Center,

71

and Casa Grande all agree
that it's just what the mall
needs. So why were my
friends and I so _incredibly_
nervous about approaching
the mall manager?

Kristy's entry in her job diary was pretty
accurate. We had each polled our bosses and
co-workers about the day-care center, and
everybody was wild about the idea. The only
problem, apparently, would be getting the idea
past the mall manager, Mr. Morton. It turned
out that our idea wasn't all that original: as
April had said, other people had suggested
something like it more than once. The old mall
manager had always turned them down flat. So
now it was our turn, with a new manager, and
we were feeling pretty tense. I mean, it's one
thing to have a great idea, but it's another thing
to request an official okay for it.

We had decided to approach Mr. Morton on
Thursday, our day off. Ms. Garcia had told
Kristy that Mr. Morton was always in his office
on Thursday afternoons, and that he had let
it be known that during that time he was avail-

able to talk to merchants or mall customers who had problems or questions. Kristy's brother Charlie had agreed to drive us to the mall in the Thomas/Brewer van, and he arrived at our school right on time. We had all taken a few minutes after our last classes to spruce up, and I guess the effect was a little startling.

"Wow," said Charlie. "You guys look very — uh — "

"Professional?" asked Kristy. "Is that the word you're looking for?" She plucked nervously at the front of her white blouse.

"I guess it'll do," said Charlie. He still looked shocked. "Man, I can't remember the last time I saw you in a skirt," he told his sister. Kristy blushed, and looked annoyed at the attention. "But you look really nice," Charlie added hastily. "And so do the rest of you. Great tie, Logan."

Now it was Logan's turn to blush as he looked down at the blue-and-red striped tie he was wearing with a white shirt and corduroy jacket. "I borrowed this from my dad," he said. It seemed like a good idea to wear one. We agreed to dress as if we were going on a really important job interview — not that any of us have actually *been* on a job interview before." He laughed.

I had to admit we were a pretty spiffy-looking crew. Claud and I had chosen conservative dresses with nice pumps and traditional accessories: no wild jewelry or wacky hairstyles. Mary Anne looked demure in a navy-blue dress with a white collar, and Jessi and Mal had both worn skirts with new sweaters.

We didn't talk much during the ride to the mall, partly because we were feeling nervous but mostly because we had already spent so much time talking about the day-care center. We had agreed, during the bus ride home the day before, that Kristy would be our spokeswoman. She had rehearsed her speech and knew exactly what she was going to say.

Charlie pulled up at the mall entrance and dropped us off. "I'll be waiting here in an hour," he said. "Good luck!"

We jumped out and headed for our first stop: the security office. It's on the main floor, down a hall near the food court, back where the mall bathrooms are. Kristy had told her boss, Ms. Garcia, that we would stop by to check in and get directions to the manager's office.

"My, don't you all look nice," said Ms. Garcia, after Kristy had introduced us. She was a small, wiry woman with black hair and flashing brown eyes. "I'm sure Mr. Morton will be impressed." She turned to the little girl by her side. "This is my daughter, Kellie," she said. "Her baby-sitter had to cancel today, so Kellie came to stay with me after school."

Kellie, who had the same dark eyes and hair as her mother, looked about six. "Having fun, Kellie?" asked Kristy, bending down to talk to her.

Kellie shook her head. "Uh-uh," she said. "It's boring here. Mom won't let me do *anything* but sit and watch her work."

"This office isn't a great place for kids," Ms. Garcia admitted. "And I don't want her wandering around the mall by herself. Meanwhile, I haven't gotten a thing done this afternoon. You can see why I support your idea."

"How about if we take Kellie with us to Mr. Morton's office?" Kristy suggested. "It'll free you up to work, and she might be able to help us convince him that this center is just what the mall needs."

"Great!" said Ms. Garcia. "Want to go, Kellie?"

"Sure," Kellie answered. I guess hanging out with a bunch of teenagers sounded like more fun than sitting in an office with her mom. She grabbed Kristy's hand. "Can we get ice cream after?"

Kristy glanced at Ms. Garcia, who shrugged and nodded. "Well, maybe," said Kristy. "We'll see."

"Mr. Morton's office is near the end of this corridor," said Ms. Garcia, leading us to the door and pointing down a hall. "It's the third door on the left." She patted Kristy on the back. "Good luck!"

I have to say that walking down that hall was one of the most nerve-wracking experiences I've had in a long time. We seemed to feel more and more nervous the closer we got to that third door on the left. Kellie clung to Kristy's hand, and it looked to me as though Kristy was clinging right back. Mary Anne and Logan were also holding hands, and I noticed that Mary Anne's knuckles had turned white. Jessi and Mal were biting their lips, and Claud was toying with her (fake) pearl necklace. As for me, well, I was feeling kind of light-headed, which made me wonder if I would have to break out my insulin kit right there in the manager's office. What if my blood sugar went crazy when Kristy was in the middle of her pitch? Thinking about it made me even more anxious, so I tried to distract myself — and the others — by starting a conversation about a movie playing at the mall that week.

"Did you guys see that movie poster?" I asked.

"I not only saw the poster," said Jessi, "I've seen the movie. Ten times. It's not so great."

That was the end of that. I tried to come up

with another subject, but my mind was blank. It didn't matter, though, because by then we had reached the door and we were clustered around it, shooting nervous glances at each other. "I don't know if I'm ready for this," said Kristy. "I mean, that last manager sounded really mean. What if Mr. Morton hates the idea and just kicks us out? Then we'll have to go tell everybody we failed."

That didn't sound like Kristy. She's not usually a worrier.

"We can still back out," said Mary Anne. "I mean, it's not like we actually have an appointment or anything. He'd never know if we just turned around and left right this minute." She looked as if she wanted to bolt.

But then, Kellie sealed our fate. She reached up and banged on the door. "Knock, knock," she cried. "Anybody home?"

"Oh, my lord," Claud said under her breath.

Kellie giggled, as if this were a big game. The rest of us looked at each other wide-eyed. "We can't leave now!" whispered Logan. Then we heard footsteps, and the door swung open.

"Well, hello," said the man who had opened the door. "What have we here?"

He was friendly looking, dressed in jeans and a white shirt. He folded his arms and looked us over. "Can I help you with something?"

None of us had said a word yet. He must have thought we were nuts, standing there silently in our perfectly pressed clothes.

"Uh — we're looking for Mr. Morton," said Kristy. "The mall manager?"

"You've found him," replied the man. He stuck out his hand. "Ted Morton, at your service." I was surprised — he was much younger than I expected.

Kristy stuck out *her* hand, and they shook. "Kristy Thomas," she said. Suddenly, she sounded more like the Kristy I knew. Confident, secure, and ready to take on the world. "These are my friends," she went on. She introduced us all, including Kellie. "We were wondering if you might have some time to talk to us about a project we have in mind."

"Of course, of course," he said. "That's what I'm here for." He opened the door wide. "Come on in," he went on. "I don't know if I have room for everybody to sit, but please try to make yourselves comfortable."

He led us into his office, which was messy, with files and stacks of papers spread out all over the desk. There were only a couple of chairs, and Kristy grabbed the one nearest to his desk. Mr. Morton sat in his own chair, behind the desk. The rest of us leaned against the cabinets or just stood near the wall. I took Kellie's hand and stood with her next to a copy machine that sat in one corner.

Mr. Morton leaned back in his chair and smiled around at us. "You look like an enterprising bunch of kids," he said. "Tell me about your project."

"Well," said Kristy. "It's more of a business than a project. See . . ." She began her speech. She told him about Project Work, and a little about the BSC. Then she started to explain about the day-care center, and why we thought it would be a good idea. At one point, she interrupted herself to introduce Kellie and tell him why she was with us, and then she went back to explaining how we thought the center could be set up. She told him that a group of store-owners were already ready to take responsibility for running it, probably so he wouldn't be able to dismiss us as just a bunch of kids. "So that's it!" she said.

Mr. Morton was silent for a few beats. Then he grinned at Kristy. "I like it!" he said. "I like it a lot. It's a terrific idea."

I let out a breath I had been holding for what seemed like five minutes.

"I had a feeling you'd like it," said Kristy. "I mean, being a parent yourself, I knew you'd understand."

"Parent?" repeated Mr. Morton. "I'm not

even married. I don't have kids."

"Oh!" said Kristy. "I thought you did. I've seen you on the security videotapes a bunch of times, talking to some kids. I just assumed they were yours."

"Nope!" he said. "Not mine. Probably, um, just some young customers . . ." He stood up and started to pace around a little. He looked excited. "Okay, here's the deal," he said. "I have an empty storefront by the games arcade. I'll let your group use it for half of the regular rent. If you can convince your bosses — and the other merchants — to come up with the rest of the rent, you can have your center."

"YESSS!" shouted Kristy, pumping her fist in the air. Then she caught herself. She looked down and smoothed her skirt, blushing. "I mean, thank you very much. That's great news."

Five minutes later, we were at the ice cream parlor and Kellie was licking a chocolate cone. In fact, we all treated ourselves (I ordered pure fruit sherbet) and had a regular celebration. Everything had happened so fast, we could hardly believe it. But it was definitely not a dream. Our day-care center was going to become a reality!

CHAPTER 9

"Phew! There sure is a lot to do," said Kristy, looking over a sheaf of papers that April had just handed her. It was the following Tuesday, and we were in the middle of our second planning meeting for the day-care center. All the members of the BSC were there — our bosses had agreed to let us take extra time off for the meetings — plus April and two other store-owners who had agreed to help us start the center.

April had left her part-time employee, a woman named Sarah who usually works Fridays, Saturdays, and Sundays, in charge of Toy Town. She and I had hurried over to the store that would soon house the day-care center, where we had met the others. Mr. Williams, who manages the Cheese Outlet, was there, and so was Ms. Snyder, who's a salesperson at Lear's, the main department store in the mall. Both of them had already talked to April about wanting to help, and they were eager to get started. But April had been the most enthusiastic. She had spent the last few days running around doing research.

The papers Kristy was looking over were regulation lists and application forms that April had picked up from the people who are in charge of licensing for day-care centers. "I guess this isn't something you can just casually jump into," Kristy said now, after she had read through some of the material. "There's a lot to figure out. Like, if kids are going to bring food with them, we'll need to have a refrigerator. And that's the least of it. We also have to hire enough staff to cover the requirements for kids at all different age levels. Plus we have to set up different areas for babies, toddlers, and school-age kids. *And* there are a *ton* of health regulations."

"We can do it," said April. "It's just a matter of working through these forms and setting things up correctly." Then the licensing people come and do inspections, and after that we'll be on our way."

Mary Anne looked around the room we sat in. It was a big rectangular space, with a storeroom and a bathroom in the back. The walls were a sort of dingy light green. "At least there's plenty of room," she said. "But this place sure could use some sprucing up. Painting with bright colors would help a lot."

"I think our next step should be making up a list of things we'll need," said Ms. Snyder. "Paint is an example, and so is the refrigerator. Then we can try to get donations from the merchants. I've already talked my boss into the idea of Lear's donating some used office equipment — we'll need a desk and a file cabinet."

"I spent some time last night writing a note about how the center will work," said Mr. Williams. "I hope you all don't mind. I think it will help a lot when we present the idea to the other merchants." He passed around a letter he'd written. It outlined the idea of the day-care center, which we had worked out during a short meeting the day before. The center would be run as a co-op. Store-owners who were interested in being part of it would get together to pay the rent each month, at least at first. Hopefully, once the center was running, it would make just enough money, through fees charged to parents, to cover the rent plus the salaries of the employees. The center wouldn't operate to make a profit. We agreed that the fees should be as low as possible, so it would be affordable for everyone.

"This looks great," said Logan, after he had read through it. "I'll bring one over to Casa Grande and ask my boss to pass it around."

"I'll take one, too," said Jessi. "My boss is pretty excited about this."

Mr. Williams had plenty of copies of his letter, and we all took a few to pass out.

As my friends and I left the meeting, I noticed that Kristy looked a little down. "Is something wrong?" I asked her. "I mean, everything seems to be going well, don't you think?"

"Oh, things are great with the day-care center," said Kristy. "But right before the meeting we had our own meeting in security. I was so sure that the shoplifting would stop after we caught those kids, but it hasn't."

"That's what Ms. Munro told me," said Mal. "She said stuff is still disappearing. Not from the bookstore so much, though. It's mostly little things, like from the drugstore."

"That's right," said Kristy. "Except it's not only little things that are being stolen. What Ms. Munro may not know is that some big things have been reported missing, too. Things like computers and VCRs. They've been taken during the night, and somehow they're getting past the security cameras."

"Maybe they didn't catch all the shoplifters last week, after all," said Logan.

"No," said Kristy, looking miserable. "They're sure they did. They interviewed all those kids, and they're positive about it. The thefts happening now are being done by someone else."

"What's security going to do?" asked Claudia.

"Keep on reviewing the tapes, I guess," said Kristy. "And they're going to put on more patrols."

I was glad to hear that. Knowing that major shoplifting was still going on made me nervous.

Back at Toy Town, I took over the cash register while Sarah slipped out for a quick break. April had stayed behind to talk to Ms. Snyder and Mr. Williams for a few minutes. When she came back, I asked her what she knew about the thefts.

"I heard about them," said April. "But nothing's been taken from here. Not big things, and not little stuff, either. As far as Toy Town is concerned, the shoplifting is over, thank goodness. But Cindy Snyder was just telling me that she heard some strange things have disappeared from Lear's — towels, she said, and a pair of boy's jeans that were on display. And she mentioned something about some sweaters, in kids' sizes. And three camcorders disappeared last night from that electronics store, and they can't figure out how they were taken. They were in a locked storage room."

I shook my head. "It's too bad," I said. "I

hope security can get to the bottom of this. I don't like the idea of thieves wandering around in the mall."

"You and me, both," said April. "Now, how about if we get some of this stock unpacked and priced?" She handed me a magic marker and a box of stickers, and showed me a price list that matched the contents of a large carton of merchandise. Then she went off to run the cash register.

For the rest of that week, I was a little nervous whenever I worked at Toy Town. I tried to get my tasks done and watch for shoplifters at the same time, but it wasn't easy. It didn't help that April had to bring Sandy on Wednesday, and I ended up watching him, too. Not that I really minded: Sandy and I were getting along very well by then. But still, it was hard to give him the attention he needed and also keep an eye on every customer in the store.

By the following week, I was feeling a little calmer. Things were still disappearing from other stores in the mall, according to Kristy, but the shoplifters seemed to be avoiding Toy Town. Some food had been stolen from the Cheese Outlet, and some hairbrushes had been taken from the Dollar Store — but nobody seemed interested in stealing toys. A few big things had been taken, too: a treadmill, and a large-screen TV. Whoever was doing the shoplifting sure had strange habits.

Meanwhile, our plans for the day-care center were going well: we had already signed up enough store-owners to more than cover the rent, and donations of equipment and supplies were coming in every day.

On Tuesday afternoon, we had a short meeting in the empty store. Mary Anne brought in some paint samples she had gotten from the hardware store, and we looked them over. We planned to paint the main walls white, and then use bright, primary colors to block out areas for different age groups. We were going to have a painting party that weekend (on Sunday, when the mall was usually a little quieter), and we hoped to get a lot of the work done then.

Claudia had drawn a plan of the room, and it looked terrific. "See, where this red stripe is will be the toddlers' area," said Claud, pointing to a corner where we could set up a table and small chairs for coloring, a trunk for dress-up clothes, and an area for block constructions. "And we'll put the babies over here," she went on, "in the blue corner."

"The HomeStore has already offered to donate five high chairs and three cribs," said Jessi, checking her notes.

"And I'm going to donate a bunch of these

great animal mobiles I have," said April. "Babies love them."

The biggest area, which Claud had colored green, was for the school-age children. We planned to have two play tables there, plus a small library of books (the BookCenter would be donating those), an arts-and-crafts area, and a "quiet" corner, where kids could be by themselves.

After the meeting, April and I headed back to Toy Town. The store was busy, and a long line of customers was waiting to check out. April went right behind the counter to work with Sarah at the register, and asked me to help a short, blonde woman who appeared to be looking for something in the doll section.

"Can I help you find something?" I asked the woman.

"Oh, I hope so," she said. "It's my niece's birthday tomorrow, and she's got her heart set on one of those dolls that comes with a book. I think it's called *Baby Read to Me*, or something like that."

"*Baby Tell Me a Story*," I said. "I'm so sorry, but I think we're all out. That doll has been very popular."

"Oh, dear," said the woman. Her face fell.

"Wait a second," I said, remembering something. "A shipment might have come in this morning. Let me go check." I ran to the back of the store and into the stockroom. *"Baby Tell Me a Story,"* I muttered to myself, as I searched through the boxes that were stacked on the shelves. "I'm sure April said they came in. Now where are they?"

I moved a carton of Legos aside to check behind it, and there on the shelf was a big case of the dolls I was looking for. I grabbed it and pulled it down, intending to open it on the floor and take one out. Just then I heard a noise behind me, and I turned around quickly.

Standing between me and the door to the store, was a man. A man in a dark red ski mask that completely covered his face.

"Oh — " I began to say. My heart had jumped into my throat, and my knees felt weak.

"Don't say a word," the man interrupted me, in a brusque voice. He ran toward me, and for a second I thought I was going to pass out. But then he pushed by me and ran out the back door of the stockroom, the one that leads into the mall. He ran silently — I guess because he was wearing sneakers along with his blue jeans and light blue shirt — pulling off his mask as he went out the door.

Five minutes later, I was sitting in April's tiny office, shaking like a leaf and giving my report to the guards from security. "Did anybody catch him when he ran out?" I asked.

One of the guards shook his head. "Nobody saw anything unusual," he said. "I guess once he took the mask off, he looked like everybody else in the mall."

That was a scary, scary thought. Here was a possibly dangerous criminal, wandering through the mall looking just like any other shopper. I felt someone rub my shoulder, and glanced up to see Kristy, looking sympathetic and also very important, her security walkie-talkie pressed to her ear.

"We'll get him," she said, patting my shoulder again. Now she looked grim. "I promise you, we'll get him."

CHAPTER 10

Ten minutes later, I had finally stopped shaking. I was still sitting in April's office. The security guards had left, but Kristy had stayed with me.

All of a sudden, I put my hand to my mouth. "Oh, no!" I said.

"What?" said Kristy, reaching for her walkie-talkie. "Did you just remember something about the guy? Wait — I'll call Pete so he can take it down." She was on a first-name basis with all the security guards.

"No, no," I said. "It's not that. It's *Baby Tell Me a Story!*"

"*What?*" asked Kristy. She looked at me as if she thought I had gone off the deep end.

"It's a doll," I said. "This customer was looking for it." I headed into the store, Kristy following me. "April," I said, "did that woman get her doll?"

April smiled at me. "She sure did," she said.

"It's nice of you to remember. You're a great salesperson." She gave me a quick hug. "Now, why don't you get out of here? I think you have a bus to catch. Go home and try to relax for the rest of the day. Everything will be all right." She hugged me again, tighter. "I'm so sorry it had to happen," she whispered into my ear.

"It's not your fault," I said.

"I know," she replied, letting me go, "but I still feel kind of responsible. I mean, I keep wondering if I locked the stockroom doors properly. How did he get in there, anyway?"

Kristy stepped in. "Whoever this guy is, he probably has no problem getting into any of the stockrooms in the mall. I'm sure you didn't do anything wrong. And believe me, security is on the case. It won't be long before we catch him." She sounded confident, but I wondered. So far, security seemed totally baffled by the new batch of thefts.

I said good-bye to April, and Kristy and I headed for the bus. As we left Toy Town, we saw Claudia walking toward us, munching a cookie covered with M&M's. "Hey!" she called, waving the cookie at us. "I got off a little early, so I thought I'd treat myself." She held out a bag to us. "I got enough for everybody," she went on, "and I even got some pretzels for you, Stace." Then she took a good look at me. "Stacey, what's the matter?" she cried. "You look terrible. What happened?"

"I'm okay," I said. "It's just that — " Suddenly I felt shaky again. Kristy jumped in to explain what had happened.

"Oh, Stace," said Claud, giving me a hug. "That's *awful!*" We walked arm in arm toward the exit, where we found the rest of our friends waiting for the bus. I saw Mal give me a questioning glance, and Mary Anne looked concerned, too. Claudia and Kristy told the story again, without waiting for anyone to ask me what was wrong.

"I can't believe it," said Mal, with a shudder. "How totally creepy!"

"I wonder if that's the same guy who broke into Casa Grande," mused Logan. "My boss said somebody was in there a few nights ago. Whoever it was, he didn't steal anything, though. He just used our stove to cook up a batch of burritos or something. He cleaned up after himself pretty well, but it was obvious he had been there."

"Weird," said Jessi, looking thoughtful. Just then, our bus pulled up and we piled into our regular seats. Alan Gray had given up fighting us for them; instead he usually sat in the front, along with two girls who were working at Rita's Bridal Shoppe. The back two rows of seats felt like home. Claud and I would sit in the left hand, furthest-back seat, and Kristy and Logan would alternate days sitting with Mary Anne in the right-hand back one. Mal and Jessi always sat in front of Claudia and me, and Kristy — or Logan, depending on whose day it was to sit with Mary Anne — would sit in the seat across the aisle from Jessi and Mal. Once we were all in our places, we'd make ourselves comfortable, setting our backpacks on the empty seats in front of us and stretching our legs out into the aisles.

That day, as the bus started up, Claud passed out the cookies — and handed me some pretzels — and we began to talk. I was still feeling a little shaky, but I was feeling something else, too. Determined. "We have to figure out what's going on at the mall," I said. "I can't keep working there if I have to be worried about running into thieves."

"Don't you think we should let security handle it?" asked Mary Anne, with a glance at Kristy.

"I know they're working on it, but maybe they could use some help," I said. "After all, we're there three days a week. If we really put our minds to it, maybe we can figure out how to catch the thief."

"Count me in," said Logan.

"Me, too," said Kristy. "I mean, security has all that high-tech camera equipment and everything, but I have to admit it doesn't seem to be doing much good. Ms. Garcia reviews the tapes every day, but she never sees anything suspicious. And stuff just keeps disappearing, mostly at night. I know she'd be really impressed if I came up with some answers."

"I wonder if the guy I saw today is the only thief," I said. "I mean, does he work alone?"

"If he does, he's covering a lot of ground every night," said Mary Anne. "I mean, shops all over the mall have reported stuff missing."

"It's almost like somebody is *living* at the mall," Jessi blurted out. She and Mal were turned around so they were facing Claudia and me. "I mean, first I heard about somebody sleeping in the theatre, and then Logan said somebody was cooking in Casa Grande's kitchen."

"Whoa!" said Kristy, sitting up in her seat. "I think you're onto something there. As a matter of fact, I've noticed some strange things, too. Like, the other day I was checking the bathrooms, and I found a tube of toothpaste sitting on one of the sinks. I wondered about it, but I was pretty busy, so I forgot to mention it to Ms. Garcia."

While the others talked, I was thinking about all the things that had been stolen. The camcorders and TVs made sense — they were big, expensive things that could be sold. But what about the things that April had told me about, the stuff that had been taken from Lear's? I tried to recall what she had said. Towels, I was sure. And kids' clothes. Why would a thief take kids' clothes? I told the others what I had remembered.

Everybody looked stumped, and no wonder. It just didn't make sense. Then, suddenly, Mal's eyes lit up. "I know! It's those kids!" she said. "The ones who came to my first story hour. There was something strange about them. They weren't carrying jackets. And I didn't see a parent pick them up — just their older sister. I've seen them a bunch of times since then, too. They're always around. I bet they're living at the mall."

"But why?" asked Mary Anne. "Why would a bunch of kids be living at the mall?" She took a bite of her cookie, which she had been nibbling at, and chewed thoughtfully. (Everybody else had already devoured theirs.)

"I don't know," Kristy answered. "But I think Mal is onto something. What do the kids look like, Mal?"

"They're blonde," she replied. "And a little grubby. Kind of skinny."

"That's them!" said Kristy. "The kids I've seen on the videotapes. The ones who were talking to Mr. Morton. I'm almost positive."

She stroked her chin. "Hmmm. . . . I wonder if he knows anything about this."

"Well, don't go bothering him with a whole bunch of questions, Kristy," said Claudia. "He's being so nice about the day-care center — we don't want to do anything to upset him."

"I won't," said Kristy. "Anyway, we don't have any proof about this. Mr. Morton would think I was nuts."

"So what do we do now?" asked Jessi.

"Keep our eyes open, I guess," said Mal. "We're just guessing about those kids. I mean, even if they are at the mall a lot, that doesn't mean they're actually *living* there. And if they are, and they've been taking things like towels, that doesn't explain the *big* stuff that's been stolen. I mean, what would those kids do with a *treadmill*?"

Claudia nodded in agreement. "Besides, what about the guy Stacey saw? He sure wasn't a kid. So far, this doesn't really add up. There are still a lot of questions."

Everybody was quiet for a few minutes, and I sat there looking out the window and thinking about the guy in the stockroom. I knew it would take me a long time to forget the sight of the man in a ski mask. I wondered if we were doing the right thing, getting involved in this mystery. I really hoped we could help solve it, but it could be dangerous. I mean, if it was only about kids living in the mall, that was one thing. But that seemed to be just one small part of the puzzle. Something else was going on, too, something serious. The only thing I was sure of was that I did not want to run into that guy again anytime soon.

The bus was driving through Stoneybrook by then, and I watched as we drove by the elementary school. The playground and playing field were empty, since it was almost suppertime. I thought about some of the kids I usually sit for, and realized that I had been missing them — especially Charlotte Johanssen, who is like a little sister to me. As much as I liked Project Work, I realized, I'd be happy when it was over and I could return to my life of school and baby-sitting. Baby-sitting is hard work, but all I could think about as I sat there on the bus was how *simple* and uncomplicated it usually is. I mean, you may have to deal with a dirty diaper or two, but shoplifters and burglars in ski masks don't enter into the picture.

When we reached SMS, my friends and I jumped off the bus. I was still feeling a little upset, and Claud noticed. "I'll walk you home, Stace," she said.

"That's okay," I said. "I'm all right. All I need is to go home and have supper with my mom. I just want to forget the mall for a while."

"Are you going to tell your mom what happened today?" asked Kristy.

"I don't know," I said. "I guess not. She might ask me to quit working at Toy Town, and I don't want to. I want to be at the mall with all of you, and help set up the day-care center and everything. And I *really* want to solve this shoplifting mystery, so things can get back to normal."

"It'll be okay, Stace," Kristy assured me. "We won't do anything dangerous."

"That's right," said Mary Anne. "We're just going to keep our eyes and ears open."

"But do me a favor," said Claudia, "so I don't have to worry about you." She grinned at me. "Stay out of that stockroom, okay?"

I nodded. "You don't have to tell me *that*. From now on, if somebody wants *Baby Tell Me a Story*, she'll have to go get her herself!"

CHAPTER 11

"Let's see. The Perkins girls all have colds, Buddy Barrett won a prize for his science project, and Jamie Newton is in a play at his preschool," said Shannon. It was Friday, and we were in Claud's room, having a BSC meeting. Shannon had been writing in the club notebook regularly, but none of us had had time to read it, so she was filling us in on what was happening with our regular clients.

"It sounds like you've been really busy," said Kristy. "I hope you're not *too* overwhelmed."

"Oh, no, I'm enjoying it," said Shannon. "Answering the phone is no problem, since I'd be here anyway. And sitting so much is a nice change from my regular routine. Plus, the kids are so cute. I think Shea Rodowsky has a crush on me."

"Really?" asked Claud, grinning.

"Yeah," said Shannon. "He's been writing me poems and everything."

"I miss Shea," Kristy said with a sigh. "I even miss Jackie."

Jackie Rodowsky is Shea's younger brother, and he's a great kid except for the fact that he's extremely accident-prone. Sitting for him is mostly a matter of damage control.

The phone began to ring then, and we spent some time setting up a few weekend jobs.

"So, what's going on at the mall?" asked Shannon, when Kristy had hung up after arranging a job with Mrs. Hobart.

"What *isn't* going on at the mall?" replied Kristy. "It's been a madhouse. First of all, we're still working on setting up the day-care center. And we're all involved in our jobs. On top of *that*, we're trying to solve this mystery. You won't believe what happened to Stacey yesterday."

We gave Shannon the details, and her eyes grew rounder and rounder as she listened. "Wow!" she said, when we had finished. "So what happens next? Do you guys have a plan?"

"Not really," I said. "We just want to try to figure out what's going on."

"I've been thinking about it," said Kristy, leaning back in the director's chair and adjusting her visor, "and the more I think about it, the more I wonder about Mr. Morton. He might be involved somehow. There's just something about him that makes me suspicious. I'm always seeing him on the videotapes, talking to those kids. Plus, he seemed so jumpy when I mentioned that I thought the kids belonged to him. He changed the subject fast and started to pace around the room, remember?"

Jessi nodded. "Also, he gave the okay for the day-care center awfully fast. He didn't take much time to think about it. That made me wonder about him. I mean, he didn't stop to look at a budget, or anything like that. And the rent for that storefront is a lot. I saw it on some of the paperwork. How can he afford to lose fifty percent of that every month?"

"I know," Mal admitted. "But I didn't want to question it. I was so happy he said yes. Besides, he seems like such a nice guy. And why would he be involved in stealing from the mall? After all, he *is* the manager. Shoplifting makes him look bad."

"Whoa!" I said. "Speaking of looking bad, I just remembered something. A while ago there was an article in the paper about the mall. Something about how it was in financial trouble, maybe even on the verge of going bankrupt. It never happened, so I forgot about it, but if something *was* wrong, maybe Mr. Morton was involved."

"I smell a rat, as Watson would say," said Kristy. "This is definitely something to check out."

"Okay," said Mary Anne. "How can we find out more about the mall's finances?"

"No problem," said Claud. "All we have to do is go to the library tomorrow and look up back issues of the newspaper. My mom can help us if we get stuck." (Mrs. Kishi is the director of the Stoneybrook Public Library, and she's guided us through this kind of research more than once.)

"Jessi and I won't be able to come," said Mal. "We're sitting for my brothers and sisters, remember?"

"Logan and I kind of have a date," said Mary Anne. "But we can cancel it. We were just planning to go on a picnic."

We convinced Mary Anne to keep her date, and Shannon, Kristy, Claud, and I agreed to meet at the library at noon the next day.

We whipped into action as soon as we arrived at the library. Claudia, who's an ace with the microfiche reader (she *is* a librarian's daughter, after all) had the machine all ready. Shannon pulled out a pad and pencil for taking notes, and Kristy and I read over

Claud's shoulder as she ran the machine.

"I guess we look up Washington Mall," said Claudia. She ran through a few pages until Kristy stopped her.

"There!" she said, pointing. She read off a date, and Shannon noted it down. "And there's another," said Kristy. "But these articles are really recent. They're probably about the kids who were arrested. We need to look further back."

Ten minutes later, we had a whole list of dates to check out. One by one, Claudia found the articles on the microfiche and we read through them. Sure enough, the recent ones were about the wave of shoplifting at the mall, and how the problem had been "solved" by the arrests of five teenagers. But when we looked at the articles from several months before, we "hit paydirt," as Kristy said.

First, there was a piece about how the previous mall manager, Ms. Richards, had retired. It mentioned that Mr. Morton had been promoted to the position. Before that, he had been some kind of assistant manager. Next, there were a whole bunch of stories about new and exciting happenings at the mall, such as a book drive that was held to benefit a homeless shelter in Stamford, and free Sunday concerts for kids. Mr. Morton seemed to be the driving force behind the "new, community-minded spirit at the Washington Mall," according to one reporter.

The next articles we read weren't quite so upbeat. One raised the question of a "misappropriation of mall funds." And the next two discussed the possibility of the mall filing for bankruptcy. The second one even referred to the fact that Ted Morton was being investigated, though it wasn't clear why.

"Whoa," said Shannon, looking over the notes she had made. "This doesn't look so good. Your Mr. Morton sounds like he's into some bad business."

"I know I was the one who suspected him first, but now that I see these articles, I don't want to believe it," said Kristy. "I mean, he's such a nice guy. And he's done a lot of good for the mall — and for the community."

"True," said Claudia, as she turned off the microfiche machine and leaned back in her chair, "but there's obviously something funny going on."

"It still doesn't add up, though," said Shannon. "I mean, what about those kids you mentioned? Where do they fit in?"

We looked at each other and shrugged. Our research hadn't made anything clear — in fact, as we left the library that day, we only felt more confused.

* * *

The next day, Sunday, my friends and I headed over to the mall for the painting party. Charlie drove us in Watson's van. "You guys sure look different from the last time I saw you," he said as he dropped us off. It was true. That afternoon, we had been dressed in our best clothes. This time we were wearing stuff we'd found in the rag-bag. Claudia, for example, had wrapped a neon-pink bandana around her head, and she was wearing a humongous pair of overalls over an ancient striped T-shirt. "Didn't you know?" she asked Charlie with a grin. "This is the latest fashion. We're always on the cutting edge."

The painting party was a blast. April had supplied a tape player, and everybody had brought along their favorite cassettes. Mr. Williams surprised us with some cool old rock from the 60s, and Ms. Snyder's choice, classical music, was actually pretty nice to paint to. We divided up the room into sections and split up our group into teams, and then everybody got to work. I was in the toddler corner with Claudia and Ms. Snyder, while Kristy, Mary Anne, and April worked in the baby area. Logan, Jessi, Mal, and Mr. Williams were painting the older kids' section.

By noon, we were splattered with white paint, and the walls were nearly covered. We decided to eat lunch while we waited for the first coat to dry. Claudia nudged me as we unwrapped our sandwiches, and when I followed her glance I saw Mr. Williams offering some crackers to Ms. Snyder, with a look on his face that could only mean one thing. "I think he has a crush on her," Claud whispered to me. We giggled.

After lunch, I worked with Kristy and Mary Anne. We talked a lot (quietly) about Mr. Morton and the mystery at the mall, but none of us had come up with any new ideas. "I wish I could slip into his office and go through his files," said Kristy. "I could probably get the key to it at the security office."

"Kristy, you can't do that!" I said. I was so shocked I almost knocked over our bucket of paint. "That's probably illegal, and it's definitely wrong."

"I know," she admitted. "I didn't say I *was* going to do it. I just said I *wished* I could."

I knew what she meant. The mystery was frustrating. We were just going to have to keep our eyes open and wait for something to happen.

CHAPTER 12

JOB DIARY......Jessi Ramsey

Today I had to deal with something I was totally unprepared for. My boss, Mr. Magee, has told me how to cope with teenagers making out in the back row (shine a flashlight on them), people who talk during *the movie (ditto), and kids who run up and down the aisles (threaten to kick them out). I thought I was ready to face anything that might happen in the movie theatre. But there was one thing Mr. Magee never covered....*

On Tuesday, Jessi went to work at Cinema World knowing that she would have a busy day. A birthday party was going to be held that afternoon at the theatre, and she was supposed to help supervise it. Cinema World has a special program called the Movie Club. When you join, you get a membership card, and every time you go to the movies, you show your card and the ticket-taker punches it. When you have ten punches, you start getting special discounts on tickets, free popcorn, and stuff like that. For kids ten and under, twenty punches on their Movie Club card means that they can have a Movie Club Birthday Party.

The birthday girl or boy can invite up to ten guests to the party, and all the guests get to see the movie at half price. Afterward, the party moves to the Movie Club room (a small room off the lobby), where the kids can pig out on free popcorn and sodas.

Jessi's first task was to decorate the Movie Club room with the streamers, tablecloths, and party hats that Mrs. Powers, the mother of the birthday girl, had brought in. The kids — a bunch of six-year-old girls — were already watching the movie when Jessi arrived, and she only had fifteen minutes to get the room ready.

"Hannah *insisted* on these Ninja Turtle decorations," said Mrs. Powers, who was hovering around "helping" Jessi. "I wanted to do something tasteful, with a nice color scheme, but no. She had to have Ninja Turtles." She held up one of the tablecloths and sniffed.

"I think it's neat," said Jessi. "A lot of girls only like Barbie or the Little Mermaid. Hannah must be pretty special."

"Oh, she is!" said Mrs. Powers, her eyes lighting up with pride. "You should hear her read out loud to her little sisters. She's only in first grade, but she's already reading at a fifth-grade level!"

Jessi, whose back was turned to Mrs. Powers at the moment, raised her eyebrows. She wondered if the proud mama wasn't exaggerating just a bit. But all she said was, "That's great!" She shook out the other tablecloth and covered a table with it. Then she stood on a chair to attach one end of a streamer to the wall. Mrs. Powers was still just standing there, holding the first tablecloth and talking about her wonderful Hannah.

"Uh-huh, uh-huh," Jessi said, pretending to listen to every word. She stepped down from the chair and checked her watch. The kids would be descending on the room within minutes. Jessi rushed around setting out soda and cups and putting up the rest of the streamers, and finally the room was ready. "Excuse me," she said to Mrs. Powers, who was still talking. "I'm just going to go get the popcorn. I'll be right back."

By the time Jessi returned with the popcorn, the ten kids were in the room, and the noise level was *high*. Hannah sat at the head of one of the tables, a huge pile of colorfully wrapped presents in front of her. She eyed them with pleasure. Her little sister, who looked about three, sat near her, squirming with excitement. "When are you going to open them, Hannah?" she kept asking. "Open mine first!" Most of the other kids were running around yelling a phrase from the movie they'd just seen: "Ooohhhh, nooooo, not the alligators!" they shrieked. Mrs. Powers stood in the center of the room, looking as if she had a bad headache.

"Anyone for popcorn?" Jessi said, in a voice loud enough to be heard over the din.

"Yea!" the kids yelled. They rushed to sit down at the tables. Jessi scooped popcorn out of the big bag she'd brought and dumped it into plastic bowls. She passed the bowls around, and suddenly the room became a lot quieter.

"You're very good with children," said Mrs. Powers as she and Jessi stood watching.

"I've had a lot of experience," replied Jessi. She told Mrs. Powers a little about the BSC, and before long Mrs. Powers had pulled out a notepad and was taking down Claudia's number.

"We have another daughter, too," said Mrs. Powers. "Lea. She's only one and a half, though, so she's with her aunt today. It's hard enough having Emily here, when she's so much younger than the others." She nodded toward Hannah's little sister, who had spilled most of her popcorn on the floor.

"Soon there'll be a day-care center at the mall," said Jessi. "It'll be perfect for this type of situation. If it was here already, you could have dropped both of your younger girls off there, and they'd be having a terrific time."

"What a wonderful idea," said Mrs. Powers. "I must say, this mall is certainly changing for the better lately."

Just then, Emily started crying over her spilled popcorn, Hannah began asking if it was time to open her presents yet, and three of the girls at the second table started a popcorn fight, giggling madly as they tossed handfuls across the table.

"Whoa," said Jessi, "I think it's time to start the games."

Jessi had already set out some games the Movie Club kept on hand. She'd found Twister and Pin the Tail on the Donkey, and a small tape player and some cushions for Musical Cushions. (That's a version of musical chairs which is a lot less likely to end in tears: instead of kids losing out as the chairs are taken away, the object of the game is for everybody to try to squish close enough together to fit on nine cushions, and then eight, and so on until everybody's all packed together on one little cushion. There's always a ton of giggling during Musical Cushions.)

"What would you like to play first, Hannah?" Jessi asked.

"Twister!" cried Hannah. "And I get to spin the dial!" She ran to take the dial from Jessi, and the other girls lined up to play. Just as Hannah called out the first directions — "Right foot, yellow!" — Jessi heard a loud clanging noise coming over the loudspeaker mounted in a corner of the room.

"What is *that*?" asked Mrs. Powers, putting her hands over her ears. The noise was deafening.

"I'm not positive," said Jessi, "but I think it's a fire alarm." She was trying to sound calm, but she felt terrified. Her boss had never given her instructions about what to do when the fire alarm went off, and there she was with a room full of young children. She took a deep breath, whispered "don't panic" to herself, and began to organize the kids. "Okay," she shouted over the clanging. "We're going to line up by the door now. Quick! Whoever's on line when I count ten will get an extra container of popcorn."

Mrs. Powers seemed to come to life then, and she helped Jessi herd the kids toward the door. Then, as Jessi rounded up a couple of stragglers, the clanging stopped and a voice came over the loudspeaker.

"Please evacuate the mall immediately," it said, over a crackly background. "A fire alarm has been sounded, and the mall must be evacuated. Please proceed calmly to the nearest fire exit."

"Nearest exit?" asked Mrs. Powers, a little wildly. "Where — ?"

Just then, the door flew open and Mr. Magee popped his head in. "Follow me," he said. "The exit's right down the hall."

Jessi sighed with relief. She had no idea where the nearest fire exit was, and would not have been able to answer Mrs. Powers' question. But now all she had to do was get the kids moving and follow Mr. Magee, which was no problem at all. Except that Hannah, at the last minute, decided that she had to save her presents. She dashed back down the hall and into the room, and Jessi dashed after her.

"But my presents!" Hannah wailed, as Jessi steered her gently toward the door. "I didn't even get to open them, and now they'll all burn up!"

Jessi didn't try to answer that. She knew she couldn't waste time saving presents in a burning mall, but she didn't want to scare the birthday girl. "Let's go," she said. "I bet your mom and sister are wondering where you are." She hurried Hannah to the exit door which Mr. Magee was holding open. Then she and Hannah stepped outside into the bright sunlight.

"Over here, Hannah!" called Mrs. Powers, who was standing near a lightpost with the group of children. Hannah ran to her.

Jessi, blinking, turned to look at the mall. She didn't see any flames or smoke, and she wondered if there really was a fire.

"Hey, Jessi!" I shouted. I had seen her come out, and now I ran to meet her. Mallory joined us.

"Do you think there's really a fire?" Jessi asked.

I shook my head. "I don't think so," I said. "I've already talked to Alan Gray and Logan, and to people from a couple of stores, and nobody saw or smelled anything."

"Must have been a false alarm," said Mal.

We stood talking for a while. Fire engines pulled up, and the fire fighters jumped out and ran into the building, but nothing else happened. They didn't come back to get hoses or anything. On the other hand, they weren't about to let us into the mall until they were positive there was no fire.

After about fifteen minutes, Mrs. Powers told Jessi that she and the girls were going to leave. "I'll drop by later to pick up the presents," she said. "But I think for now we'll just continue the games at home. Thanks for all your help."

Jessi said good-bye to Hannah and the rest of the girls, and then we stood around and waited some more. Finally, Kristy showed up, looking important in her security cap.

"False alarm," she said, without our even having to ask. "And I already saw the video-tape from the camera posted near the box."

"Wow, really?" I said. "What did you see?"

"Nothing conclusive," said Kristy. "But there was one weird thing. Right after the alarm went off, those three blonde kids ran past the camera. And they looked scared to death."

CHAPTER 13

"Ahh!" said Kristy, flopping back on my bed. "This is great. Just like we planned — no work, no baby-sitting, no meeting. Total relaxation." She picked up my copy of *#1 Fan*, a magazine I sometimes buy, and started to leaf through it.

Kristy, Mary Anne, and I were hanging out at my house after school on Thursday. We had been looking forward to this afternoon ever since we had planned it, weeks ago. Project Work had been taking up a lot of our time, but there was only one more week to go. Then we'd return to our busy schedules of school, sitting, meetings, and more sitting. For just this one afternoon, we had planned to take it easy. Later, Kristy was going to Mary Anne's house for dinner and my mom had offered to take me out to my favorite restaurant.

Claudia had an art class that afternoon, and

Mal was sitting for her brothers while her mom took the girls shopping. Logan had track tryouts, and Shannon was sitting for the Rodowskys. Jessi had planned to spend some time with Becca, working on a garden they were planning for the Ramseys' backyard.

Mary Anne leaned over Kristy's shoulder to look at the magazine. "There's Cam Geary," she said. "Doesn't he look gorgeous in that blue shirt? Blue is his favorite color, you know." Mary Anne has had a major crush on Cam Geary for a long time. She's always telling Logan he looks just like Cam.

"Is that why you bought Logan a blue shirt?" Kristy asked.

"No!" exclaimed Mary Anne, blushing. "Well, maybe that was partly why. But blue happens to be Logan's favorite color, too."

I picked up another magazine. "Cam's okay," I said, "but he's kind of young. I like older guys, like Steve Matthews." I showed my friends a poster-sized pullout of a guy with dark hair and deep brown eyes.

Kristy threw down her magazine. "I don't know," she said. "None of these guys seems real to me. I mean, I'd want to know how well they can catch a line drive to third base. That kind of thing matters more to me than looks."

"I guess Bart's perfect for you, then," I said.

"I've seen him do some amazing things on a baseball field." Bart Taylor is Kristy's sort-of boyfriend. He coaches a softball team for little kids, just as Kristy does. Sometimes Kristy's Krushers and Bart's Bashers play each other.

Kristy sighed loudly.

"Thinking about Bart?" asked Mary Anne.

"Not really," Kristy said. "I'm thinking about what we're *all* thinking about, even though we don't want to admit it. I'm thinking about what's going on at the mall."

Mary Anne and I looked down at the floor. It was true. As hard as we were trying, we couldn't really relax and forget about the problems at the mall.

"Let's just talk about it," said Kristy. "There's no point in pretending we aren't worried about them."

"Them" — the three blonde kids. Since Tuesday, when Kristy had seen them run past the video camera after the alarm had been pulled, none of us had spotted the kids even once. We didn't see them leave the mall on Tuesday, after the fire alarm. And we didn't see them anywhere on Wednesday. And they hadn't shown up at Mal's story hour, which was unusual, since they had been coming regularly. They didn't appear even once in the videotapes Kristy had reviewed late Wednesday afternoon.

Now Kristy stood up and started to pace around. "It's so weird," she said. "I didn't even realize how much I was used to seeing them. They *always* showed up on the tapes at one point or another. Some days I'd see them four or five times. First they'd be sitting near the fountain, and then I'd see them walking through the food court — they were just, like, always *there*. And now they aren't."

Mary Anne frowned. "I hope they're okay," she said. "What could have happened to them?"

"What if it has something to do with the fire alarm?" I said. "After all, that's the last time we spotted them."

"Do you think they pulled it?" asked Mary Anne.

"They've never caused trouble before," said Kristy. "They wouldn't pull it just for fun."

"Maybe they thought they saw a fire," I said.

Kristy snapped her fingers. "I just remembered something," she said. "On that videotape — the one from the camera by the fire alarm? — guess who I saw right *before* the alarm went off and the kids ran by? Mr. Morton. He looked pretty upset, too. I didn't think much of it. He's the mall manager, and he's always showing up on the tapes."

"But you said you used to see him talking to those kids all the time," I said. "And we agree something's not quite right about him. What about the problem with the funds at the mall — that whole bankruptcy thing?"

"I wonder if he was talking to them that day," said Kristy slowly.

"What if he was?" asked Mary Anne. "He's a nice guy, right? So, he talks to people at the mall. Why should that mean anything bad?"

Kristy sat down on the floor, and I stood up and took her place pacing around the room. I was thinking about Mr. Morton. I went over everything we knew about him. He had only managed the mall for a few months. He was a really nice, likable guy. He was willing to do all kinds of things to improve the mall and its image. The mall was in financial trouble.

"I wonder if — " Mary Anne began, but I interrupted her.

"Whoa!" I said. "I think I just figured it all out!" I stood stock still, next to my desk. Mary Anne and Kristy looked shocked. "Well, maybe not all of it," I went on. "But listen. I think I know what's going on. You know how everybody says Mr. Morton is such a nice guy? Well, that's the problem."

"What do you mean?" asked Kristy.

"What's wrong with being a nice guy?" asked Mary Anne.

"I'll tell you," I said. I started to pace again, around and around. Past the desk, past the closet, past the bureau, past the bed. Then I started talking fast. "That's how he got himself — and the mall — into such a mess. He's such a nice guy that he can't say no to anybody. He wants to do everything he can to help the mall and the community. So he says yes to benefit concerts, special discount programs, and even day-care centers."

"But those are all good things," said Mary Anne, looking confused.

"I agree." I stopped pacing and stood near my current favorite poster (it's a photo of a basset hound with a funny-sad expression). "But they cost money. In order to do those things, Mr. Morton must have run through all the money in the mall's account. Then maybe he started to, well, 'misappropriate funds,' like it said in the newspaper, to cover up his mistakes."

"Ohhh!" said Mary Anne. She was beginning to look excited.

"And *then*," I went on, "it came out that the

mall was close to bankruptcy. So he couldn't play around with the accounts anymore. But he didn't want to start saying 'no' to everybody. So then — "

"So then he started stealing things!" said Kristy, jumping to her feet. "All those big things, the camcorders and the treadmills and the wide-screen TVs!"

"Oh, no!" cried Mary Anne, putting her hand over her mouth.

"Oh, yes!" said Kristy. "Stacey, you're a genius! This explains everything. Mr. Morton *must* be the one stealing that stuff, because he's the only one who would know how to get around security to do it. He'd know how to dodge them on their rounds, and even how to avoid the video cameras so he wouldn't show up on tape."

"He couldn't have stolen all those big things by himself, though," said Mary Anne.

"No, he must have people working for him. People who would know where to sell the stuff, and people to help him take it. Like that guy you ran into in the stockroom, Stacey." Kristy was really excited now, and so was I. Mary Anne just looked dismayed. She can't stand to think the worst of anybody, even if it's somebody she barely knows, such as Mr. Morton.

"The guy in the stockroom," I mused, remembering that scary, masked face. Then I had a terrible thought. "Maybe those three kids are working for him, too!" I said.

"Oh, no," said Kristy. "He wouldn't do *that*. Too risky. I mean, that's really serious business, getting kids involved in a crime."

"But what if," Mary Anne said slowly, "what if the kids found out what he was doing?" She glanced up at me, and I saw how frightened she looked.

For about thirty seconds, there wasn't a sound in my room. Mary Anne sat staring at her hands. I looked at the basset hound poster, without really seeing it. And Kristy plopped down on the bed again and just sat there, frowning.

"If they found out," I said finally, "I guess Mr. Morton would be pretty scared. Maybe pretty angry, too."

"He'd have to do whatever it took to keep them quiet," said Kristy in a low tone.

"And now they're missing," Mary Anne whispered.

There was another silence.

"Maybe they're just hiding," I said hopefully, after a minute. "Washington Mall is huge, but they probably know every inch of it by now, if they really are living there. I bet they'd know how to stay hidden."

"That's right," said Mary Anne, grabbing at

the chance to feel optimistic. "They're probably hiding."

"I hope they are," said Kristy. She stood up, and suddenly she looked full of energy. "But I'm not counting on it. It's time we found out. We have to get to the mall right away!"

CHAPTER 14

"I'll call Charlie and see if he can give us a ride," Kristy said.

"Who else can help us?" I asked. "We need all the people we can get."

"I bet Claudia's back from art class by now," said Mary Anne. "And maybe Jessi can come. Mal and Shannon are both sitting, though, and I doubt Logan is done with his tryout yet."

We got busy making phone calls, and before long Claudia and Jessi had joined us at my house. Two minutes later, Charlie (good old Charlie) had pulled up in Watson's van. He honked the horn and we came running out.

On the way to the mall, Kristy explained everything.

"Don't you think you should consider going to the police?" asked Charlie. "This sounds serious. I mean, there are three kids missing."

Kristy thought for a minute. "Okay, how's this?" she asked. "I don't really want to get the police involved unless we have to. I think it would scare those kids if they saw cops searching the mall, and they might hide themselves even better. How about if we give ourselves a deadline?" She glanced at her watch. "It's three-thirty now. If we don't find them by five-thirty, we'll call the police."

"Good idea," said Jessi. "I have to be home no later than six, anyway. I left Becca with Aunt Cecelia, on the condition that I would get home in time to help with dinner. So, let's synchronize our watches, like on TV."

"Okay." Claudia checked her Swatch and announced that she was already synchronized with Kristy. The rest of us made sure the time on our watches matched theirs.

Charlie pulled up at the mall entrance. "I'll drop you off and go park," he said. "I'll catch up to you, wherever you are. I want to help find those kids."

We ran into the mall and gathered near the main escalators. "I've been thinking," I said. "We have to be careful about this search. I mean, we want to find the kids as soon as possible, but we don't want to scare them off. Also, we don't want to make anybody suspicious, especially Mr. Morton."

"That's right," said Kristy. "Plus, we don't know if anybody else at the mall is working with him. So we can't assume that anyone is trustworthy."

"We have to work fast, and work quietly," said Jessi. "No problem. Should we split up into teams?"

"That's a good idea," I replied. "We *do* have a lot of ground to cover. How about if Claud and I start on the top floor and work our way down, while you and Kristy and Mary Anne work from the main floor up?"

"Okay," said Kristy. "What are we waiting for? Let's go for it! We can check in with each other at Critters in, say, half an hour?"

The search was on. I felt as if I were in one of those adventure movies in which the hero has to find a bomb within one hour, or else it will blow up the whole city. You know, the kind of movie where they show a clock ticking away the minutes, and you feel more and more tense as the minute hand moves nearer and nearer to midnight? Well, in our case the minute hand was moving nearer to five-thirty. Here's how our search went:

Three-forty: Claud and I headed into the Cheese Outlet, and Mary Anne, Jessi, and Kristy hopped onto the escalator. In the cheese store, Mr. Williams was glad to see us and wanted us to taste some free samples. "We're in kind of a hurry," said Claud. "But thanks."

We glanced around the store, but didn't dare ask Mr. Williams if he had seen the kids. What if he were working with Mr. Morton?

Three-fifty: We checked the upstairs bathrooms. Charlie showed up just in time to look into the men's room. Report: no kids, but some sign of them. Charlie found a comb on the sink in the men's room, and in the women's room I found a towel — the stolen one? — draped over one of the stalls to dry. "We could be right behind them!" I said. "Let's keep moving."

Four-ten: After searching through Stuff 'n Nonsense, the candy store (I had to drag Claud away from the jelly-bean display), and Soundscapes, we were beginning to feel frustrated. Since the bathrooms, we had seen no sign of the kids.

Four-fifteen: We met up in front of Critters. Nobody else had seen any sign of the kids, either. We decided to re-form our teams and stay on the bottom three floors, where we'd spotted the kids most often. Jessi and I went down to the BookCenter, while Claud stopped in at the Artist's Exchange and Mary Anne visited her boss at Critters. Charlie and Kristy moved ahead to the food court, where we would all meet again in ten minutes.

I cruised up and down the aisles in the BookCenter, peering over displays and checking behind the puppet theatre. "Jessi!" I hissed at one point. I gestured toward a small blonde kid who I could only see from the back. He — or she — was nestled into one of the reading corners with a book. Jessi crept along one of the shelves, trying to remain hidden, until she could check out the kid's face. Just as she looked back at me and shook her head, I felt someone behind me.

"Can I help you girls?" asked Ms. Munro. "Aren't you friends of Mallory's?"

"No — I mean yes — I mean, we are friends, but we don't need any help, thank you," I stammered. "We're, uh, just looking." It wasn't a lie. We *were* just looking. We weren't looking for books, though.

Four-twenty-five: We met at a table in the food court. "Nothing to report," said Claudia. "The Artist's Exchange was pretty empty."

"Same with Critters," said Mary Anne. "I did spot Mr. Morton on my way down here, but he was on the "up" escalator. He looked kind of preoccupied."

"We have something to report," said Kristy. "According to this guy Harry, who works at Casa Grande with Logan, somebody used the kitchen again last night."

"So the kids are still around!" said Mary Anne. "What a relief."

"We still have to find them, though," said

Kristy. "And they seem to be lying low. Char-lie and I are going to check the second-floor bathrooms next."

"I'm going to go back upstairs to Cinema World," said Jessi. "Maybe I can find out if anybody slept there last night, if I ask care-fully."

"Mary Anne and I can check the women's room down here," said Claud. "Although I doubt we'll find anything there. This is begin-ning to seem hopeless! How will we *ever* find three kids in this huge mall?"

"We just have to keep trying," I said. "I want to stop in and see April. How about if we meet by the fountain in a few minutes?"

Five-oh-five: April was busy at Toy Town, so I couldn't really talk to her. But Sarah, her assistant, was setting up a display of new rub-ber stamps, and I spent some time talking to her. She mentioned that two "really polite kids" had been hanging around about an hour earlier. "I was amazed," she said. "They played with the Legos, but then they put them back neatly."

"I guess their mom came for them?" I asked casually.

Sarah wrinkled her brow. "I don't think so. An older girl stopped by — maybe their sister? — and herded them out of the store. I heard her say something about naptime."

Five-ten: "Naptime," said Kristy, when I met the others (who hadn't found any sign of the kids in the bathrooms or Cinema World) and told them what I had heard. "Where would they go to take naps?" She thought for a moment. "It would have to be someplace quiet, someplace hidden away. I know! There are some empty offices back by security. Let's check them out."

Five-twenty: After an extensive check of the offices and rooms near security, we had found absolutely nothing. Kristy led us through a maze of hallways that I had never known about, but every room was empty.

"What are we going to do?" wailed Jessi, looking at her watch. "Our time is almost up."

"Naptime," I muttered to myself. "Naptime." Suddenly I snapped my fingers. "I've got it!" I said. "Those mats the Exercise Shoppe donated for the day-care center! They're piled up in the back room of our storefront."

Five-twenty-eight: We were off and running almost before I had finished my sentence. But as we approached the day-care center, its door and windows soaped up until the center was ready to open, Kristy held up her hand. "Hold on," she said. "We better do this carefully, so we don't scare them away. If they take off now, we'll never find them in time."

133

She seemed so sure that they were in there. I wasn't as positive, but I didn't have any better guesses. "Do you still have the key, Kristy?" I asked.

She nodded. "I've had it ever since the painting party," she admitted. "I forgot to turn it in to Ms. Garcia."

"Good thing," Charlie said. "Now, are there any nearby exits from the store?"

"One," said Mary Anne. "Down that hall." She pointed.

"I'll head down there and guard the door," said Charlie.

"Maybe a couple of us should guard this one, too, while the others go in," said Mary Anne. She and Jessi decided to stay by the door.

Five-thirty-one: "It's okay, we're on your side," Kristy was saying. She and Claud and I had opened the door as quietly as possible, tiptoed through the storefront, and entered the back room.

There, sound asleep on the mats, were the two younger children. The older girl sat nearby, reading a copy of *A Wrinkle in Time*. She was the one Kristy was talking to. When we entered the dimly lit room, she looked up in alarm. There was no time for her to run, though, so she just stayed seated, staring up at us with frightened eyes.

"Are you all right?" asked Kristy. "We were worried about you. We haven't seen you in days."

"We're — we're fine," said the girl. "How did you know about us?"

"We've been working at the mall," I explained. "And we've seen you around. I'm Stacey, by the way. This is Kristy and this is Claudia."

"I'm Mara," said the girl. "And that's Kyle," she pointed at the boy, who was sitting up and rubbing his eyes, "and Brenda." Brenda sat up too, and yawned. "I'm twelve, Kyle's eight, and Brenda is six."

"And you live at the mall, right? Why?" asked Kristy bluntly.

"It's kind of a long story," said Mara.

"In that case, let's go get the others," I said. "They'll want to hear it, too."

A few minutes later, we were all gathered in the back room, seated on mats. And Mara began to tell her amazing story.

"We haven't lived here for very long," said Mara. "We used to live in those apartments over on Sycamore Street, with our mom. We never had much money, but we got along." She swallowed. "But then Mom had to go to the hospital. And my aunt was supposed to come take care of us, but she never showed up. I didn't want to worry my mom, so I just

135

decided we could take care of ourselves. We did okay for a while, but then the money she left ran out, and the electricity got turned off, and the rent was due. I knew the landlord would be coming around, so we had to get out of there fast. This was the only place I could think of." She blurted out her tale so fast my head was spinning.

"We didn't steal anything," said Kyle, suddenly. "I mean, nothing we didn't need, anyway. And we were going to pay the stores back as soon as we could."

"We didn't steal big stuff, like Mr. Morton," added Brenda. Mara shot her a warning glance.

"You knew about him?" I asked.

Mara nodded hesitantly. "But then he found out about us, too. He found us sleeping in the movie theatre one night. From then on, we sort of had an agreement. We wouldn't tell about him if he wouldn't tell about us. It really seemed like he wanted to help us, too. Anyway, it worked fine until last Tuesday."

"What happened then?" I asked, leaning forward. My heart was beating fast. Finally the pieces of the puzzle were beginning to come together.

"I guess he started to worry that we would tell on him. He kind of threatened us," said Mara, looking scared again.

"Yeah, but I showed him," Kyle spoke up proudly. "I pulled the fire alarm and shut down the whole mall. That way we had time to find a bunch of new hiding places, so he could never find us."

"But what — " I began. I had about a million questions to ask them. Just then, I felt somebody tugging on my arm. It was Kristy. She pulled me away from the group and started talking in a low voice.

"We have to call the police," she said. "I know we might get the kids in trouble, but this is not something we can handle on our own. Anyway, Mr. Morton has to be stopped."

I glanced over at the three scruffy kids who were talking with my friends. I was kind of in awe of them for surviving on their own. But they needed help — more help than I could give them. I knew Kristy was right.

CHAPTER 15

"I, um, need to call my mother," I said, when Kristy and I had rejoined the group. And it wasn't a lie. I really *did* need to call my mom. She was planning to take me out to dinner, and she'd be wondering where I was.

"I should call home, too," said Mary Anne. "Kristy was supposed to come over for supper tonight. I better tell them we'll be late." She stood up to join me.

"I'm hungry!" Brenda wailed all of a sudden. "*I* want dinner."

"Shhh!" whispered Mara. "We'll eat later, when everybody's gone."

"In the kitchen at Casa Grande?" asked Kristy. "I had a feeling you guys were the burrito banditos." She was trying to keep the tone of the conversation light, but Mara still blushed a deep red.

"We used their kitchen because it was the easiest to get into, out of all the places on the

138

food court. We were going to pay them back as soon as we could," she said earnestly. "And we always cleaned up after ourselves." She looked down at her hands.

Mary Anne touched her shoulder. "It's okay, Mara," she said. "Everything's going to be okay." Mara gave her a timid smile.

"Let's get these kids something to eat," said Charlie, springing to his feet. "Do you like cheeseburgers, Kyle?"

"Oh, wow," said Kyle, grinning. "I *love* them."

"Great," said Charlie. "And I bet *you* like fries, don't you?" he asked Brenda.

She nodded shyly. "With ketchup!" she said.

"You don't have to do this," Mara said to Charlie. "We'll get by. Really."

"No way am I missing out on a cheeseburger," said Kyle, frowning at her. "I'm *sick* of burritos. Come on, Mara, *please*?"

"Okay," said Mara, nodding to Kyle. Then she turned to Charlie. "But we'll pay you back as soon as we can. That's a promise."

Charlie stuck out his hand, and they shook. Then he looked at me, and I knew *he* knew I was planning to call the police. "Why don't you and Mary Anne go make your calls," he said, "and we'll meet you at Friendly's. In, say," he checked his watch, "fifteen minutes?"

He gave me another Look, and I nodded. He wanted to be sure I would let the police know where to come and when to get there.

"See you!" I said, waving to everybody. "Better order me a grilled cheese. I'm starving. Oh, and Jessi, I'll call your aunt Cecelia for you," I added.

"And I'll have a cheddar burger," said Mary Anne. "Well done."

Kristy pretended to write our orders on an imaginary pad. "Coming right up!" she said. "See you!"

Mary Anne and I took off toward the phones near the main entrance. On the way, I explained what was up. She wasn't surprised. "That's what I thought," she said. "I hate to do that to the kids, after they've put so much energy into surviving on their own. But the fact is, they need help."

When we reached the phones, we both called home first and explained that our dinner plans were off. Then I called the Ramseys, and then the police, which was one of the hardest things I ever had to do. "We'll send somebody right out," said the person who answered the phone. After that, Mary Anne and I ran over to Friendly's.

We found our friends and the three kids at a big round table. Kyle was taking huge, hungry bites out of a cheeseburger, Brenda was loading fries with ketchup and wolfing them down, and Mara was taking tiny, polite bites of a tunafish sandwich, the cheapest thing on the menu. She looked up at Mary Anne and me and smiled — and then she looked past us and her body stiffened. I turned around and saw a policewoman approaching the table.

Mara looked as if she wanted to take off running, but she held her ground. She shot fierce looks at Brenda and Kyle, as if warning them to let her do the talking. The police-woman pulled up a chair. "Are you Mara?" she asked. I had given the police her name.

Mara nodded, looking frightened.

"Don't worry," said the policewoman. "I'm Lieutenant Shay — you can call me Irene — and I'm here to help you."

Mara didn't look convinced.

"Why don't you tell me your story?" Irene asked gently. "And then we can figure out what to do next." She took off her hat and stuck it on Kyle's head, which made him grin.

Mara started talking, slowly at first. Then she built up steam and the words spilled out. My friends and I leaned toward her, listening as eagerly as we had the first time. I had never heard anything like the story Mara told. She added some details we hadn't heard the first time: about how she and Brenda and Kyle had only moved to the area a few months ago, and hadn't enrolled at school yet. That was one reason nobody had missed them. And how they hadn't had a phone put in yet — because they couldn't afford it — which was why their mother couldn't call and had no idea that they weren't in the apartment where she'd left them. They'd visited her a few times, using coins fished from the fountain for bus fare, but they never told her where they were living. "She was just so, so sick," said Mara. "I couldn't stand to add to her worries."

It turned out that the strongest force driving Mara to do what she did was her fear that if the child welfare people got involved, she and Kyle and Brenda would be separated. "But I guess now that's going to happen anyway," said Mara. She looked at me, and I knew she felt betrayed. She had probably figured out I was the one who had called the cops.

Once she had finished telling Irene how she and Kyle and Brenda had survived in the mall, Mara stopped talking. Brenda filled in the silence with a little made-up song about her french fries.

"Isn't there something else you want to tell me?" asked Irene, after a minute or so. She had been taking notes while Mara talked, and now she looked Mara in the eyes. "Something about the expensive merchandise that's been disappearing at night? We know you didn't take it — none of you looks strong enough to carry away a microwave, much less a tread-mill. So what about it?''

Mara looked trapped.

''Don't worry. Nobody will ever find out who told us,'' said Irene.

Mara mumbled something about Mr. Morton, and then began to speak more freely. Irene listened closely and took some more notes. Then she took her hat back from Kyle and stood up. ''Time to go find Ted Morton, I think,'' she said. A woman who had entered the restaurant a few minutes earlier and sat at a nearby table, stood up also, and came over to our table.

''I'm Mrs. Peabody,'' she said to Mara. ''I'm a social worker with Stoneybrook Social Services. We want to help you. We have a car waiting outside. Will you come with me, please?''

And that was the last we saw of Mara, Brenda, and Kyle. As the social worker led them away, Brenda waved a french fry at us, Kyle gave us a ketchup-smeared grin, and Mara looked at us with accusatory eyes.

''I guess my favorite day would have to be the day Benny — he's the cook at Casa Grande — taught me how to make enchiladas,'' said Logan. ''I was surprised at how much fun it was. I've even been thinking lately that I might want to go to cooking school someday, and learn how to be a great chef."

It was a week and a day later, and we were gathered in Claud's room for a BSC meeting. Claud had passed around a bag of Chee•tos Paws, plus some cookies sweetened with fruit juice that are okay for me to eat. We were celebrating our last day of Project Work, and between calls from clients we were talking over what we had liked best about working at the mall.

"I loved the BookCenter," said Mal. "Maybe I'll have a little bookstore someday. I could work there in the mornings, and write in the afternoons." She looked dreamy.

"I'll run the bookstore in the afternoon," said Jessi. "It sounds like a lot more fun than working in a movie theatre. Although I do have to say I enjoyed learning how to operate the projector."

Mary Anne showed us the present her boss had given her on the last day — a red collar for Tigger — and Claud brought out the paint set she had saved for and bought from Artist's Exchange.

"My last day with security was pretty quiet," said Kristy. "It seems as though the serious shoplifting has finally stopped. We met with the new mall manager today, and he's excited about some plans he has for deterring shoplifters before they even start stealing. He's a great guy — Mr. Buford, his name is — and he has some excellent ideas for the mall. Plus, he's had lots of experience."

"What about Mr. Morton?" asked Shannon. "What's going to happen to him?"

Kristy frowned. "I guess he'll have to go to court. It's a shame, really. He did *mean* well."

"But I'll never be able to forget how he threatened those kids," said Mary Anne. "How could such a nice guy do such a rotten thing?"

We sat there shaking our heads, puzzled.

"And what about the day-care center?" Shannon asked. "Is there still going to be one?"

"Oh, definitely," I said. "April told me they hope to open within a few weeks. And guess who's quitting his job to be the center's full-time director? Mr. Williams, the guy from the Cheese Outlet."

"That's great," said Kristy. "He'll be wonderful with the kids."

"Speaking of kids," I said, "I haven't told you all the *best* news. I called Mrs. Peabody today, over at Social Services? And it sounds like everything is working out just fine for Mara and Kyle and Brenda. The night they took them away, they contacted Mara's mom in the hospital. She was almost ready to be released. Mrs. Peabody brought the kids over to the hospital and they had a really great reunion."

"So they'll be living together again, back in their apartment?" Kristy asked.

I nodded. "They're going to get some assistance from Social Services, and the family will be getting some counseling, too. I felt so much better after talking to Mrs. Peabody. I mean, turning Mara in was incredibly hard — but now at least I know that was the right thing to do."

"Wait till I call Dawn and tell her about all of this," said Mary Anne. Her eyes were brimming with tears. "It's such a great story, with a 'happily ever after' for everyone."

"Everyone except Mr. Morton," said Kristy. She looked at the clock. "By the way, it's after six," she said. "I think this meeting is adjourned."

"Then let's call Dawn right now," said Claud, diving for the phone. "I want to talk to her, too. Once she hears about our next Short Takes class, maybe she'll come back home even sooner."

"What's the next class?" asked Shannon.

"Oh, it's a great one," I said.

"It should be totally fun — and relaxing, compared to Project Work," said Kristy.

"What *is* it?" Shannon asked again.

"Something everybody really needs, after six weeks of Project Work," said Mary Anne. We all started to giggle, except for Shannon, who sat there looking bewildered. Soon we were laughing so hard it was impossible to talk, but I finally managed to squeak the words out. "Stress Reduction for Teens," I said. Then I fell back onto the bed, gasping for breath as my friends and I laughed some more.

About the Author

ANN M. MARTIN did *a lot* of baby-sitting when she was growing up in Princeton, New Jersey. She is a former editor of books for children, and was graduated from Smith College.

Ms. Martin lives in New York City with her cats, Mouse and Rosie. She likes ice cream and *I Love Lucy*; and she hates to cook.

Ann Martin's Apple Paperbacks include *Yours Turly, Shirley; Ten Kids, No Pets; With You and Without You; Bummer Summer;* and all the other books in the Baby-sitters Club series.

THE BABY-SITTERS CLUB

Look for #15

KRISTY AND THE VAMPIRES

Anyway, that afternoon Mary Anne had ridden up on her bicycle and hopped off before I even noticed. But as soon as Emily Michelle spotted her, I did, too. "Mary Anne!" I said. "Guess what?"

"Guess what?" she said at the same time, as she bent to hug Emily Michelle. "They're making a movie here!"

"That's what *I* just heard," I said. "Do you know anything about it?"

"Not much," she said. "Just that they're using a house near mine to film part of it."

"Really?" I asked. "How cool! We can go over and watch."

"And that it's a TV movie," Mary Anne continued, "and it's going to be called *Little Vampires*."

I grinned. "*Little Vampires*?" I repeated. That sounded fun.

Mary Anne nodded. "It's about a group of

boy vampires," she said. She looked thoughtful for a minute. "Do you think Cam Geary
might be in it?" she asked hopefully.

Cam Geary is a TV star, and Mary Anne has
had this major crush on him for what seems
like forever. "Oh, Cam Geary," I said dismis-
sively, rolling my eyes.

"Kristy!" said Mary Anne, looking hurt.
"This might be my big chance to meet him!"

"Okay, okay," I said. "Maybe he'll be in it.
Who knows? The important thing is, they're
making a movie here. That means the summer
can't possibly be as dull as I thought it was
going to be."

Read all the latest books
in the Baby-sitters Club series
by Ann M. Martin

Mysteries:

Don't miss out on
The All New

Fan Club

Join now!
Your one-year membership package includes:

- The exclusive Fan Club T-Shirt!
- A Baby-sitters Club poster!
- A Baby-sitters Club note pad and pencil!
- An official membership card!
- The exclusive *Guide to Stoneybrook!*

Plus four additional newsletters per year

so you can be the first to know the hot news about the series — Super Specials, Mysteries, Videos, and more — the baby-sitters, Ann Martin, and lots of baby-sitting fun from the Baby-sitters Club Headquarters!

ALL THIS FOR JUST $6.95 plus $1.00 postage and handling! **You can't get all this great stuff anywhere else except THE BABY-SITTERS FAN CLUB!**

Just fill in the coupon below and mail with payment to: THE BABY-SITTERS FAN CLUB, Scholastic Inc., P.O. Box 7500, 2931 E. McCarty Street, Jefferson City, MO 65102.

THE BABY-SITTERS FAN CLUB

__ YES! Enroll me in The Baby-sitters Fan Club! I've enclosed my check or money order (no cash please) for $7.95

Name _____ Birthdate _____

Street _____

City _____ State/Zip _____

Where did you buy this book?

- ❏ Bookstore
- ❏ Drugstore
- ❏ Supermarket
- ❏ Book Fair
- ❏ Book Club
- ❏ other_____

BSFC593